EXPERIENCE POINTS

ILLUSTRATED QUEER *SMUTTY* STORIES

D1562816

NA MELAMED

Microcosm Publishing
Portland, Ore

EXPERIENCE POINTS: Illustrated Queer Smutty Stories

© 2022 Nicholai Avigdor Melamed
© This edition Microcosm Publishing 2022
First edition - 3,000 copies - March 8, 2022
ISBN 9781648410741
This is Microcosm #673
Cover by Nicholai Avigdor Melamed
Edited by Lydia Rogue

To join the ranks of high-class stores that feature Microcosm titles, talk to your local rep: In the U.S. **COMO** (Atlantic), **FUJII** (Midwest), **BOOK TRAVELERS WEST** (Pacific), **TURNAROUND** (Europe), **UTP/MANDA** (Canada), **NEW SOUTH** (Australia/New Zealand), **GPS** in Asia, Africa, India, South America, and other countries, or **FAIRE** in the gift trade.

For a catalog, write or visit:
Microcosm Publishing
2752 N Williams Ave.
Portland, OR 97227
https://microcosm.pub/queerwerewolves

Global labor conditions are bad, and our roots in industrial Cleveland in the 70s and 80s made us appreciate the need to treat workers right. Therefore, our books are MADE IN THE USA.

Did you know that you can buy our books directly from us at sliding scale rates? Support a small, independent publisher and pay less than Amazon's price at **www.Microcosm.Pub**

Library of Congress Cataloging-in-Publication Data

Names: Melamed, Nicholai Avigdor, author, illustrator.
Title: Experience points : illustrated smutty stories / Nicholai Avigdor
   Melamed.
Description: Portland, OR : Microcosm Publishing, 2022. | Series: Queering
   consent | Summary: "Alex Mazor is a transmasculine horror artist
   struggling to make a living in Toronto. When he invites one of his
   patrons home to model for his next project, his motives aren't purely
   artistic. But Matt Connors, local fantasy geek and perpetual
   DM-without-a-party, is an unlikely model and an even stranger bedfellow.
   Follow along as their relationship unfolds, from a steamy modeling
   session to some exhibitionism at an art exhibit, and a road trip that
   pushes the pair to bring their trust to a new level. In the midst of
   exploring one another's kinks and insecurities, will they be brave
   enough to find intimacy as well? This series of unapologetically filthy,
   nerdy, artistic encounters chronicles two lives at a crossroads of
   healing and self-discovery. This high-heat four-part novella is of
   Microcosm's Queering Consent series"-- Provided by publisher.
Identifiers: LCCN 2021050270 | ISBN 9781648410741 (paperback)
Subjects: LCSH: Transgender people--Fiction. | Gays--Fiction. | LCGFT:
   Erotic fiction. | Novellas.
Classification: LCC PS3613.E444427 E97 2022 | DDC 813/.6--dc23/eng/20211108
LC record available at https://lccn.loc.gov/2021050270

MICROCOSM PUBLISHING is Portland's most diversified publishing house and distributor with a focus on the colorful, authentic, and empowering. Our books and zines have put your power in your hands since 1996, equipping readers to make positive changes in their lives and in the world around them. Microcosm emphasizes skill-building, showing hidden histories, and fostering creativity through challenging conventional publishing wisdom with books and bookettes about DIY skills, food, bicycling, gender, self-care, and social justice. What was once a distro and record label was started by Joe Biel in his bedroom and has become among the oldest independent publishing houses in Portland, OR. We are a politically moderate, centrist publisher in a world that has inched to the right for the past 80 years.

Introduction

*T*here is a passage I remember from a story I read when I was younger. A passage about an aging actress singing over a weathered gramophone.

I no longer remember the name of the story, or even the language it was written in, but I do recall how the narrator described her.

"She was beautiful once."

I didn't understand this sentence at first. But as the story went on, I realized its author meant for us to pity the actress. He wanted the reader to envision her wrinkled face, gnarled hands and love handles. She was a symbol of faded glory, existing between the pages of that book only to compliment the deteriorated scenery of a shabby boarding house.

And though I continued reading, I recall nothing else—because I was already telling myself another story.

It was the story of the actress.

I imagined how she carried herself, with her proud eyes and aura of majesty. She was larger than life in dresses from a bygone age, the rich shade of lipstick she still wore, and the powerful voice that echoed through the walls of her small, but dignified apartment like a force of nature.

This was a woman of a thousand stories, the tamest of which was still more interesting than the protagonist of a cliché-ridden narrative that compared her to a run-down building.

That actress wasn't just beautiful. She was more beautiful than ever.

So now, the only reason I remember this story at all is because it made me find the words to express how my understanding of beauty differed from that of its author.

The beauty that the aging actress embodied couldn't be found on runways or airbrushed photos. It was the rare outcome of being wholly yourself—not in the way of a marketing slogan that had packaged and commodified authenticity—but with the well-earned scars, eye bags, creases and sags of a life richly lived.

There was a time when I believed you have to be old to earn that kind of beauty. That being unapologetically earnest about who you are and what you want is a privilege reserved for those too old to be punished for it.

How many people have I heard tell me—*just wait*—wait until I'm old and I'll wear that shade of red, I'll go to that faraway place I've always dreamed of, and I'll state my opinion in an unsympathetic crowd.

It's an idea that holds a special kind of dreamy allure when you're not sure you'll live long enough to actually look in the mirror and see it.

But I'm still alive (against all odds). I'm not yet old, and I do look in mirrors and see someone I never thought I'd see when I read that half-remembered passage.

That someone is myself.

The story you're about to read isn't about me, or an aging actress. But it is about people who were a part of somebody else's scenery for too long, and who found a little more of themselves in each other.

There is only one hope I have for it—and that's for you, the would-be reader, to look up from it at journey's end a little more horny, a little more entertained, and feeling a little more yourself as well.

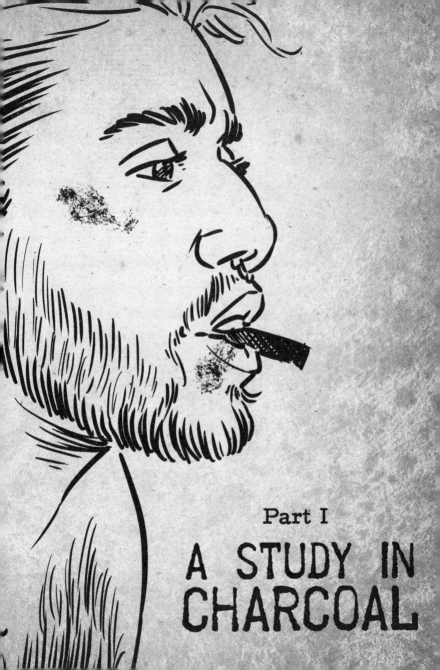

Part I

A STUDY IN
CHARCOAL

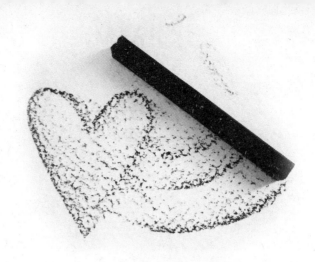

Dedicated to those of us who were
taught to feel unloveable.

THE TRUTH IS

We can love and be loved in turn.
We can be attractive.
We can choose to have sex lives.
We can take ownership of our bodies.
We can desire.
We can experience pleasure.

AND WE HAVE OUR OWN STORIES TO TELL.

I read this book once. About human brains, and how you can trace their evolution through structure, almost like rings on an old tree stump. Fleshy, misshapen rings.

Right now, some part of the pre-mammalian web that channels my soul is making a judgement about the man in front of me.

Potential mate sighted. Prepare body to fuck.

Of course, what the evolutionary biologists failed to account for is that we can't actually reproduce. Didn't account for *gay* in their little theory.

So this would be termed anomalous behaviour. Neurons misfiring. Critical malfunction detected.

Or you could choose, instead, to explain it by way of the pleasure principle. A good fuck makes for better social cohesion.

But the unasked-for rush of hormones flooding my body at this very moment tells a very different story.

It's too distracting for social anything. I can barely hear him speak over the sound of my own heartbeat.

"Hey, so this is your apartment."

I prefer another theory. Can't remember where I read it. For all I know, it's coming together on the spot as I struggle to maintain a semblance of chill.

"That's right."

An ally in mutual survival.

That's what my prefrontal cortex thinks it's spotted.

The right amalgamation of genes, read through a series of subconscious signals. Everything from the nervous way he smiles to the imperceptible emissions of his sweat glands.

Better seal the deal, it figures. Quick, do something to make his hypothalamus produce oxytocin before he gets away!

And if you think all this theorizing is making the moment any less romantic—trust me, *I'm doing my best.*

"You want tea, coffee? I've got cream."

Have I ever.

"Just water would be great, thanks."

Alright, *Mr. Just Water.*

"Well, I'll boil some water for me. Come into the kitchen. We'll talk there."

"Sure."

I feel like that dumbass teenager from *The Lost Boys*. Hopelessly clinging to anything that's nailed down before his newfound float reflex carries him through the open window. Right off into the night sky, like an anchorless balloon.

You try suppressing a homeostatic disturbance more ancient than civilization itself.

"So—"

The familiar click of the kettle brings me back to solid ground.

He's sitting at my kitchen table. Arms folded over his chest. Legs crossed. He's a fidgeter. That might be a problem.

I think it's best to jump straight in.

"Have you ever modeled before? I mean, life drawing or otherwise."

He chuckles in the awkward way of someone who thinks the answer should be obvious.

"No."

I grab a glass from the cupboard. I can feel the pressure behind me as he rolls back his memories, trying to remember something— anything of relevance.

"I think the first time was when I sat for you to get my portrait done at the fair."

I nod. Sounds about right.

"I usually hate seeing pictures of myself. Photos on Facebook. All my selfies are garbage. But I think you really—well, actually I think you drew me much better than I really look."

He looks to me for a laugh. A playful nod at his insecurities. I meet him halfway with a knowing smile.

"Is that what made you accept my invitation?"

I turn the tap. It will take a moment for the water to cool. Good.

I give him a moment to collect himself. Most people aren't used to my approach. They expect a little more small talk. A little more dancing around the point.

"Uh…"

I place the glass in front of him.

"Thanks."

"You don't have to answer if you'd rather not."

"I guess I just…" He begins, looking to the glass, as though it might offer a suitable response, "Wanted to try something new."

"It can be boring. And more than a little torturous. Sitting perfectly still for hours at a time."

"Oh yeah?" He laughs, still looking at the glass.

"Fortunately for you, I'm a quick draftsman. Which means you're free to talk. And adjust your position for comfort. Within reason."

"Good to know."

"Trust me, once the novelty of being naked wears off…"

"Um. About that."

Here it comes.

I turn to pick my mug off the counter. One bloated tea bag from this morning. I unceremoniously toss in a second. It's a weak brand, and I like the mouthfeel bitter. Oversteeped.

Finally, I look at him, "You want to keep it on?"

The simmer of the kettle almost drowns out my words. I'm evaluating him, to the sounds of whistling and steam. Looking at him, for the first time since he arrived, through the impartial eyes of an artist.

A round faced man. Probably one who would look far younger, if not for his unkempt facial hair.

I liked his eyes. They struck me as earnest. They still do.

His neck slopes into the cusp of a black t-shirt, proudly displaying a snarling beholder with a D20 on its tongue. Cute.

Tight-fitting jeans. Not so much a stylistic choice, I think, as a bad case of shrunk in the wash. My eyes linger briefly on the zipper poking out the side of his fly.

I wonder if he noticed the way my gaze drifts none-too-subtly downwards.

Finally, I pour the boiling water into my cup. The awkward shift in posture tells me he could use a break from being so closely observed.

Tell me you didn't come here to waste my time.

"Maybe...we could work up to it?"

Better than nothing. After all, I'm not paying him. This is a voluntary act. An experiment on his part.

Am I the experiment?

"I want you to feel comfortable. Do you have a favourite band? Something I could play in the background?"

"So you're probably going to think I'm a weeb—"

"You want to find the *Neon Genesis Evangelion* soundtrack on Spotify, or something?"

His eyes instantly light up.

"You've seen—"

"No, just heard. No self-respecting anime otaku of my acquaintance has ever passed up the chance to rave about it."

The hope in his eyes isn't quite extinguished, but it does fade.

I watch him get up and shuffle towards the couch. Watching for possible signs of reluctance. Watching his jeans wrinkle and distend with each motion.

I've always been deeply visceral in my approach to drawing human anatomy. Surface to surface. Compression of skin. The weight and curvature of each form as it weaves together on the page into something resembling a body.

I'm a tactile learner.

"Can we start with your socks?"

He looks startled.

"I mean—" I start to explain, but he seems to be catching up.

"Oh. Yeah, sure."

A little flustered now.

"If you'd rather change in the bathroom—"

"No. It's fine. This is fine. I mean, does it really make a difference?" He gives me that same anxious smile. I wonder if he's trying to convince himself.

His socks come off. Long toes like a Mannerist painter's wet dream. The old joke about shoe size comes to mind.

"You know, this isn't half bad."

He tries to make light of his own nervous energy.

"Right, baring your feet to strangers. Really living on the edge there." I don't mean to tease him, but I can't help it.

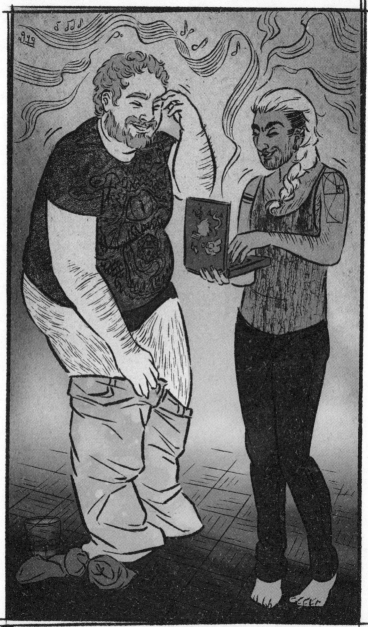

I almost feel guilty.

"I'm more arthouse. More of a Satoshi Kon kind of guy."

"You ever watched *Perfect Blue*?"

Now we're speaking the same language.

"Psychological thrillers are my jam."

His laughter sounds apprehensive.

"Yeah, somehow I can see it."

My one-track mind nurses a fantasy. I feel like the predator here. Would he like that?

I've been described as short, slight, and relentlessly intense.

This isn't the first time I've felt myself becoming a source of self-conscious dread for the larger, transparently less experienced person seated before me.

It feels good.

"So I'm all set up in the main room if you want to grab a seat on the couch. You know, shift some pillows around. Find yourself a cozy position."

I don't know why I call it that. The main room. It's all one room. Classic Toronto basement bachelor. Sometimes I think of it as the shoebox. Equal parts snug and oppressive. A shoebox I can barely afford.

"Yeah. Totally."

This temperamental wifi connection is making mincemeat of my patience. I struggle to load a comforting playlist. Something to ease his tension.

"Well fine."

Then again, this may be the right approach. Now he's a man with something to prove.

He starts to take off his jeans.

I make a point not to stare. "How's this?"

My laptop speakers flood the room with 90s anime nostalgia.

We both instinctively make the same face. With his pants halfway down his knees, a film reel of cringeworthy reverse harem anime fan service flashes past my eyes. Quickly, I move to rescue us both with some generic lofi.

"Maybe a bit much."

Our shoulders relax in unison to the halting, brooding murmur.

Good call.

"Y-yeah."

We laugh together for the first time.

This is good. This is progress.

I busy myself with adjusting the rickety easel. Unbox the charcoal. Run my fingers across the toothy texture of the page.

I even sketch a few experimental circles to loosen up my wrist.

Anything at all to give him that momentary feeling of privacy.

I hear the uncertain creak of the couch adjusting to his weight. His jeans lie discarded on the floor.

My gaze drifts along his legs. I feel their texture intimately impressing itself upon my mind. Supple hairs tracing the curvature of his calves, pressed flat against the couch cushions. He rests a hand casually against his thighs, obscuring his crotch from view. Somehow, the subtle gesture is actually more distracting than a clear view of his briefs.

"Think you can hold that position?"

He arches his back, ever so slightly, as though testing the arrangement against sore desk muscles. There is a vulnerability to the gesture that makes my lip curl.

"Probably. Is this okay?"

"If you could drape your left arm—oh no, sorry. My left. Your right. If you could—yeah that's it."

His right arm rests on his shoulder now. The fingers curl with a tender authenticity that I'm all too excited to capture on paper. Then his entire body recedes backwards into an improvised stack of pillows. Perfect.

If not for the disappointing persistence of clothing.

"You're good at this."

He makes a faint, dismissive sound.

"No, really. Some people can't pose for shit. They need you to micromanage every little thing."

"Maybe I should do this more often."

His tone suggests that he's joking, but I give him an encouraging smile.

"You should consider it."

I draft a miniature composition on my throwaway page. Then another. My model yawns.

I have an instinct for restlessness in my subjects. But even if I didn't, he's nothing if not transparently uneasy.

"It's Matt, right?"

He blinks his way into a waking state. "Huh—uh, yeah."

"Long day?"

He instantly looks sheepish.

"Actually I slept in. It's my day off."

It's tempting to ask the usual questions about work, but I resist.

Matt strikes me as the sort of man who punches the clock to sustain his passions. Short of the occasional complaint about odd hours or asinine coworkers, I doubt it's much of a topic for discussion.

"So what do you usually do on your off days? When you're not posing, half-naked, for mysterious strangers."

My delivery is dry. Casual. I get a laugh.

"Well, my friends and I recently got a group together. I'm DMing for about five people, assuming we can actually get regular attendance."

"No shit. Sounds exciting."

"Yeah. First time doing a homebrew setting! I've got the campaign mostly planned out, but there's a lot of small details about the world itself that need—"

He pauses, in the practiced way of someone who's grown used to pussyfooting around his hobbies with unsympathetic listeners.

"I mean, I don't know if you're really interested in all that."

"Taking on the worldbuilding when it's your first time maneuvering around creating your own maps and encounters seems like a real trial by fire."

He brightens. And it all comes pouring out in that familiar, ardent way of a seasoned tabletop roleplay enthusiast.

His ardor is infectious.

I find my hand swishing more rapidly across the page. Scrambling to capture that carefree vivacity before he remembers that his every arch and crease are being painstakingly scrutinized. Cut to manageable pieces.

Simplified and reassembled.

The charcoal edge lingers in rich, hefty strokes at the folded crook of his knee. The arch of his foot. The convergence of his palm and inner thigh.

It captures the abundance of his lips. The bow of his nose. The density of his eyebrows. I set to charting the slope of his neck through a carpet of disorderly wisps and dashes.

And so we have finally come to it.

"Matt?"

I catch him in the midst of explaining the finer points of a political feud between two fictional sovereign nations.

"The shirt. It's gotta go."

His expression suggests that he may have forgotten our purpose here. Realization dawns on him.

"You don't like taking your shirt off, huh?"

He seems to shrink into himself, receding further into the couch as though it might offer some measure of anonymity. The expression on his face is guarded.

"Not really."

"Alright."

I step back from the drawing and in a series of frank, deliberate motions, proceed to remove my own shirt.

He seems to be caught off guard.

"That's...more hair than I expected."

I smirk in recognition. Familiar words. Maybe it's something about being small and lithe that makes people expect a hairless body. My ego stopped flinching back from their astonishment shortly after the T kicked in.

"Not a fan?"

The self-deprecating jokes about my notoriously hairy ancestors mingle on the tip of my tongue. Apologize for your body before they turn it against you. The old habit is like hair itself, caught on my teeth and unwilling to be picked out.

I always loved running my fingers through the old body carpet. Even back in my locker room memories, before some part of me learned to be ashamed.

"Oh, no I didn't mean it like that!"

They never do.

"Then how about it?"

"I don't think you'll like what you see."

I can hear a bitter voice infringing upon my thoughts. Another ghost of the girls' locker room past:

"Thin people have it made. They're beautiful and happy, and I could be happy too, if I were thin. I know it's not rational, but—"

"Try me."

I've never seen a man get up so slowly.

It's almost theatrical. I half-expect him to raise his voice to a discordant caricature of old age and tell me something about his poor old back.

Some dark impulse makes me want to close the distance, hook my fingers to either side of his shirt and pull.

I restrain it.

He takes a breath. Makes that little "fuck it" smile to nobody in particular. Mouths the word "okay".

It's not one solid motion. He grabs and drags. A clumsy, drawn-out procedure. Longer, perhaps, than he intended. He curses as it catches on something. Painfully agitated.

I consider the weight of my next words, and how profoundly they might affect him. In my experience, compliments seldom help.

Do I appear professionally detached in that moment? Are my pupils growing wide with unmistakable appeal?

"Maybe you could just take it all off. Save yourself the trouble of having to go through striking the same pose twice over."

He's staring at the floor. I steel myself for the inevitable question. Does he have to? Is it really necessary?

"Will you?"

He asks it with a slight smile.

Now that's more interesting.

"Sure."

I begin to unbutton my own jeans. Tight by design. He raises his head. I'm not undressing in the quick, no-nonsense way of stripping off after a long day at work, but with the calculated, leisurely pace of an object of study.

Just as I'm about to shimmy my briefs off, I point with a slight nod of my head. The brief flicker of eyes. A daring smile.

Matt raises his eyebrows in acknowledgment. Then he begins to mirror my actions, like a time-delayed feed recording live.

I know that for the first few moments, he'll be too preoccupied with self-conscious thoughts of his own body to notice.

But I'm already prepared.

Not that I ever try to hide it. Not that he didn't have every possible opportunity to discover it before this moment. In my social media profile. The about section of my portfolio. Every blog interview and artist spotlight written for a local news site.

But we haven't discussed it. Not in person.

"So you're trans."

He's comfortable with the language. A good sign. Probably less explaining to do.

"Yeah."

Every moment spent struggling to wrap his mind around my body is a moment away from fretting about his own.

"Do you wanna get back into—"

"Oh, sure. Sorry."

He shuffles back onto the couch.

"Your leg was a little higher—no left, *your left*. I think because you were sat a little deeper in the—here—"

I approach him in frustration.

"May I?"

I can actually feel my insides constricting at the sudden proximity. Like a swallow caught in your throat. Hard and wet at the same time, and both equally invisible to nearby witnesses.

Advantages of being trans.

Looming over him, I correct the angle at which his arm slants between his neck and the couch.

He lets me. So I adjust a few hairs on his forehead as well. Push him back, ever so slightly, into the pillows while I'm at it.

My eyes are drawn to the hand on his thigh. The one conspiring with his posture to conceal, from my vantage point at the easel.

I meet his eyes.

I want him to know that I know.

I want to know how that makes him feel.

His face, a mask of expectant silence, makes for a welcome invitation.

I push him deeper into the pillows. Leaning into it. Leveraging his chest as a counter-weight as I clamber onto his lap. The spectre of hovering just above his penis, obscured from view by my own body, tenses my muscles in anticipatory excitement.

"I want you."

From the look he gives me you'd think he's never heard that phrase uttered outside of porn.

Or is it just that he's never heard it from a man?

I might be his experiment after all. A safe, non-threatening in between- or so his instincts led him to expect. It wouldn't be the first time.

I kiss him.

His lips are soft. The prickle of his facial hair mingles with my own. Bracingly rough. Like oversteeped tea. My fingers are tracing charcoal through his beard, but he doesn't know it yet.

I withdraw. Waggle my blackened fingers menacingly.

He laughs. "Oh no."

My thighs brush against what is decidedly no longer a semi.

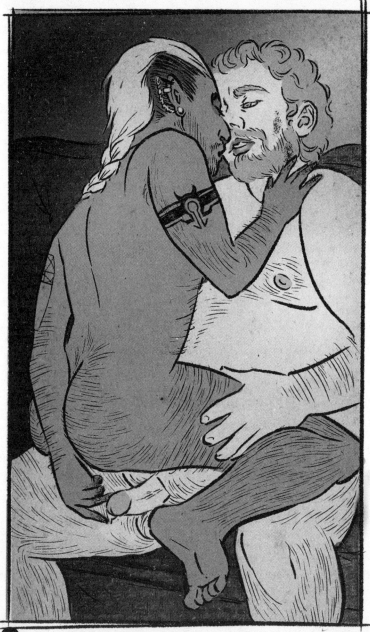

He breathes in. A sudden, sharp brush with pleasure.

"I've got a condom in my wallet."

"You always have a condom, just in case?" I grin.

"Sometimes."

Alright *Mr. Just Water.* **Mr. Sometimes.**

What a subtle, understated man you are.

"Is it in your pants?"

"Yeah. The back pocket."

I withdraw from him with care.

As I bend to rifle through his jeans, I'm deeply aware of the contour my body forms.

I want that vivid dungeon master's imagination to picture his hands squeezing my hips. Can he see himself grabbing me from behind? Pressing me down on all fours and acquainting himself with my insides?

Embossed leather shaped like a spellbook. This man is nothing if not consistent.

"Nice wallet. I think I'll be kind of disappointed if it's not one of those novelty pack condoms."

"It's Durex."

He sounds apologetic.

"You like Durex?"

"It's alright."

Something about the way he says that suggests that he hasn't exactly shopped around.

"I'm told Kimonos are good. The closest you'll get to barebacking without fear of STDs."

"Do you like them?"

"A dick is a dick. I can feel the warmth and hardness, but I think the nerve endings down there aren't sophisticated enough to tell the difference between skin and rubber."

"Huh."

So he's never bottomed. Good to know.

I can see my description is a turn on.

Warmth. Hardness. Those are good words.

I hold the condom packet within reach.

He does reach for it, but I draw back. I can't help but smile as his eyes betray something akin to anguish.

My knees buckle. I draw myself up to the edge of the couch.

"But you know, the nerve endings up here—"

I wet my lips.

"Can definitely tell the taste of sweat and pre cum from crinkly, lube-covered latex."

He breathes heavily as my tongue snakes up the shaft. I glance up just long enough to see him attempt to remain impassive

I love it when they do that. Go on. Try to stifle the appearance of being *completely overwhelmed*.

It brings out my competitive streak.

I tease the head of his penis, tracing circles with my tongue.

Covetous circles on smooth, salty skin. Slither across the veins. Taste him from side to side, like I'm committing the shape to memory. And I suppose, in a way, I am.

"Having fun, huh?"

His breathless words invite a high-pitched moan.

I swallow him whole. Let him graze the opening of my throat.

Did his balls just convulse in my palm, or did his entire body shudder?

Then I release him—slowly, haltingly. Brushing the string of saliva from my mouth with the back of my hand.

The rustle of thick, thirsty hair feels tantalizing against my moistened lips.

I rise up between his legs, extending the condom as an offering.

"I'm gonna ride you."

If you let me.

"Okay."

Something tells me I could have informed him I was about to swing acrobatically from the ceiling lamp, and he would have responded vaguely in the affirmative.

It takes a brief, expectant silence for Matt to realize that I'm waiting for him to tear the wrapper open and slip the condom into place.

I watch him roll it down his erection, still sleek and gleaming with my spit.

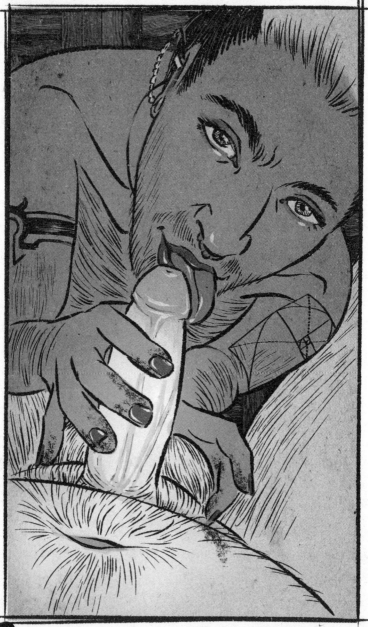

"Do you like being told what to do?"

"Are you asking if I'm a sub?"

Trans. Sub. Terms applied casually, like he's formed a sentence with them before. And yet, I sense a dearth of experience. I bet this guy has an interesting search history.

"You don't have to give it a label. Just tell me if you like it when I tell you what to do. How to pose. Where to sit. Does it turn you on?"

"Kind of, yeah."

And with that, I'm back on him. Back on his lap, pushing him back. Back into the couch.

I'm slippery against him. Hot to the touch.

Needing more room, so I make it. Enough to reach down and tease myself with his penis poised at the opening.

Something inside me stutters. Repeated convulsions, fervent and demanding. I bend forward. Lower my hips. Guide him through with deliberate force.

My nostrils flare.

He's very hard. Almost inflexible.

"Fuck."

"Does that feel good?"

"You feel—really tight."

"You're inside a muscle accordion, surrounded by walls of even firmer muscle. They like you. They don't want to let you go."

"Muscle accordion," He laughs. "I've never heard anyone use that."

I'm laughing too. "Good name, huh?"

Better than *front hole*. God, I hate that one.

It's not a fucking hole.

Do holes—swallow, pulse, contract? Are we afraid to scare people off with the truth of how lively our insides are? Afraid of the teeth and fish jokes that follow, because they make light of things that frighten them?

The lofi beats are at odds with our rhythm.

I feel him matching me. Even surpassing me.

So I slow. Forcibly. Let's not get crazy now. This is no race.

Relax. I got this.

I could use some Cage the Elephant. A little Rise Against to be my metronome. Maybe some nice, steady St.Vincent.

Masseduction. Don't turn off what turns me on.

"I want to feel you deep and slow."

My clit is swollen to full size. A demanding presence. Firm between my fingers. I stroke it slowly, in stride with my hips. In stride with the smack of his balls against my ass.

His chest heaves beneath me. He's at an incline. I can just feel his belly swell and recede against my forearm. A loose, bristling trail of hair. Framing his nipples. Trailing all the way down.

"You feel good."

"You—too—"

Our words are breathy. Everything fogs.

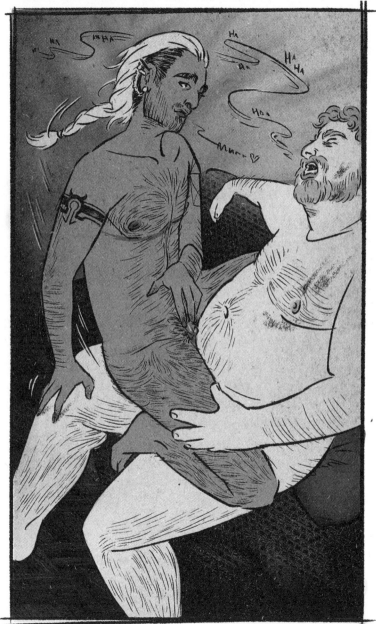

A photograph that's out of focus.

I'm gaining speed, but not with intention.

It's the momentum of my senses. The pace owns me.

A violent, indomitable urge.

Keep up. Don't fall behind. Don't falter now. Don't let me down.

He grabs me. "I'm close."

"I know."

I've got his penis in a stranglehold.

Pulled taut around the shape of him.

He feels big. Scorchingly hot inside me. I wish I could feel the spurt of hot cum. Overflowing. Free of our rubber safeguard and awash in my own cocktail of viscous, bitter fluid.

I feel the first spasm overtake me.

And then my vocal chords are on their own.

Seized by disorienting waves of ecstasy.

Practically blinded. But I keep riding him.

Harder. Faster. Clutching his body to steady myself.

Use me. Use me to finish.

He makes a pained, desperate sound.

I feel the throbbing of his orgasm, even amidst my own.

I hold his gasping body. Really feel him, wrapped up in his thundering heartbeat and climax afterglow.

It's hard not to take a certain pride in our spontaneous partnership.

We smell of sweat and sex. *A job well done.*

I draw back, noting (with amusement) that there are smudges of charcoal all across his body.

"You'd better—"

"Yeah."

I clamber off of him.

He's looking down at the condom. Still breathing heavily.

"Mind if I—"

"Go ahead."

He gets up. Stumbles a little.

I grin. "Weak at the knees?"

He chuckles appreciatively.

Confident that he'll have no trouble locating the bathroom, I make my way back towards my easel.

Now that I've been intimately acquainted with all the missing parts of my drawing, I'm eager to complete it.

My charcoal dips under the shadow of his nipples. The weighty slope of his chest to either side. A grove of bristly hairs that shape the contour of his abdomen.

I mark the hint of a nascent erection, partially concealed by the strategic placement of knees and hands.

Light falling on the couch cushion. A flyaway hair.

It's done.

The bathroom door opens behind me. I wait for curiosity to guide him. It's not until I sense my model peeking over my shoulder that I finally speak.

"What do you think?"

"You made me look hot."

I scoff.

"You are hot."

"You really believe that?"

"I fucked you."

"Fair enough."

I feel his hands on my thighs. The weight and warmth of his naked body against my lower back.

"You're pretty hot yourself."

Bristles of hair against my neck. Oh boy. Look who's riding on a wave of post-coital courage.

"Maybe you should come back again sometime. Get another hot portrait from the hot trans artist."

My tone is casual. Impersonal.

"You've got a name too. It's Alex, right?"

He wants to use my name. Fuck.

"If you're usually free on Tuesdays, maybe you could come to one of our D&D sessions. It sounds like you play."

He must sense my reluctance, because he immediately follows up with "They're pretty open-minded people."

Open-minded, huh? *Glad we cleared that up.*

My mind conjures up an image of resting cross-legged next to Matt on another couch in another darkened room, drinking beer and watching anime. Surrounded by politely awkward friends and early-2000s geek paraphernalia.

"Maybe I'll just come draw your characters."

"That would be awesome."

He means it too. I can hear the genuine excitement in his voice.

Well, most people like having their characters drawn. Most people like seeing themselves drawn. Most people like fucking.

Does Matt like me?

Fleshy, misshapen rings. Firing pleasure stimulants. Contracting my blood vessels and raising my heart rate. Flooding my body with adrenaline.

I let his hands grow bolder. Let them run, unrestricted, across my warm skin and sticky hair.

I'm still looking at the portrait. Continuing to evaluate its weaknesses, even as my mind drifts.

Have I captured the real Matt?

Finally, I turn to look at the other Matt. The one behind me.

I still like his eyes.

"I'll think about it."

Beyond Survival, How Do We Thrive?

My mind is extraordinary.

It can transform any fear into perversion.

Terrifying size can become the arms
that hold me down.

Being discounted, humiliated,
Treated like insentient garbage,
Like a thing no longer human—
In the refuge of my private thoughts,
Dislocated from reality,
Safely controlled,
It can make me shudder with desire.

I hold the reigns on my fantasy.
The finger on my trigger.
It proceeds at my pace,
And ends abruptly at my command.
I cut the keys that turn my lock.

So *why*.

When you're   so far away.

When I left you behind so long ago.

Why do I still see you

In the warm faces that surround me?

I imagine grabbing the cheap hotel lamp.

Weighted in my grasp, A bludgeon.

Such delicious carnage.

Am I the predator now?

Or am I still the prey?

Part II

SAINT
SEBASTIAN

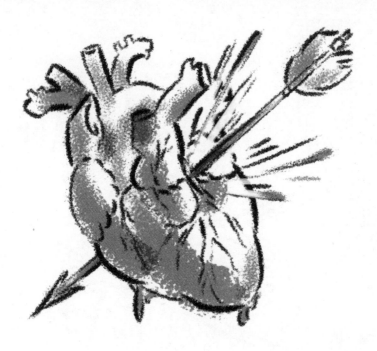

Dedicated to those of us who were

taught to feel afraid.

WE ARE

More than a slur spoken in passing.

More than an object of illicit desire.

More than a way to vent their anger.

We are deserving of protection.

AND THEIR GAZE CANNOT DIMINISH US.

T straighten my back, feeling the ligaments of my spine snap in long-awaited relief. My thumb swipes the cracked surface of the phone screen. The autumn wind relieves my sweat. Let's hope that eyeliner isn't trickling down my cheek. Sherbourne station is suffocatingly hot compared to the chill of oncoming rain outside.

Close now.

My message is an apology.

I'm running late. Devising a story about the ills of public transit to avoid admitting that mere hours ago, I was formulating excuses not to come at all.

The phone vibrates as I'm halfway to slipping it back in my pocket. More of a whimper than a healthy buzz.

See you soon :)

That was quick. I didn't expect a response.

Shouldn't Matt be preoccupied with his roleplay session?

Either he's a very distractible DM, or they're dawdling between half-baked character sheets and a table covered in convenience store snack food.

I entertain the idea that they might be postponing on my account. But didn't I tell him that I'd be a silent observer?

God, I hope they're not waiting up.

The thought carries a bitter aftertaste of guilt. The image of a door opening to five expectant pairs of eyes, scrutinizing their overdue guest.

As if I need another reason to manufacture my escape.

I clatter my way down the street, avoiding cigarette butts and construction pylons. Mountains of forbidding concrete loom to either side. My hands catch droplets. Still shy of a storm. My heels catch familiar cracks in the sidewalk.

This is no stomping ground for thigh-highs. Especially when they're matched with fresh stubble. A history of cat calls and close calls wafts through my mind.

I used to live here. Familiar mantras rise to the surface.

Hold your head high. Don't meet their eyes. Don't invite them into your life. Keep walking. You'll be fine. Keep walking.

But this time, I'm blissfully alone.

I savour the distant roar of traffic. The flicker of street lamps. The humid air that sticks in my nostrils, tasting of pot and raw sewage.

The lights are on in the apartment lobby. I can see my reflection in the dark glass of the security camera. Somebody brushes past me. A tall man, wearing a tuque and heavy parka. I catch the door on his way out.

No guard or nearby busybody to reprimand the gesture, so I'm in. Pressing the button. Waiting for the distressing clank of a nearby elevator.

Once the metal doors slide shut behind me, and the floor number glows a foggy yellow, I make a point of avoiding the judgemental gaze of my endlessly reflected selves to either side.

Hlurk. Ack. Kerchunk. It lives.

I catch enough of a glimpse to fix my hair.

Unsuccessfully, I think.

At least there's no smear of pigment to darken the bags under my eyes. My linework has survived the sweat. Good buy, for war paint salvaged from the drug store clearance aisle.

And I am certainly at war tonight.

It takes a while to find the right door. One of those circular hallways with hypnotic floor patterns and esoteric conceptions of numeration.

I knock before I call him.

There's a muffled sound, releasing me from the otherworldly stillness. I've never been in an apartment hallway so quiet. They must have thick walls around here.

Then it dawns on me. Is that the SNES theme to Super Ghouls 'N Ghosts? I can't help but break into a stupidly wide grin. Pure nostalgia for the era. That game was torture.

I'm almost disappointed when it ends.

"I'm here."

"Oh, yeah sorry I'll be right down—"

"No, I mean—"

The door swings backward. I stumble against the wall to prevent him from barrelling through me, presumably on his way to the elevator.

"I mean right outside."

His mouth begins to form the shape of a second apology, but he's struck dumb, taking it in.

The floral print shirt, revealing my unshaved chest. The leather jacket, covered in last year's button haul from a local zine fair.

Skin tight jeans stuffed into lace-up boots. My garden of piercings. My half-assed Siouxsie Sioux eyes.

"You look- different."

"Bad different—or good different?"

"Just- different."

Articulate as ever.

"Well, you look pretty different yourself."

I guess he's one of those people who likes to dress up for tabletop roleplay. He's got a young Deckard Cain thing going on. The scraggly beard really works for this look- bonus points for actually being real.

"Yeah it's—" He looks embarrassed.

"No, it's cool. I have a thing for wizards." I have a thing for wizards? As in, hey Gandalf, why don't you show me your real staff? Wow. Get it together, Alex.

He laughs nervously. Doubly embarrassed now.

"Uh, actually I was gonna say it's kind of a waste, since pretty much everyone cancelled last minute," He's trying to look stoic about it, even with the hurt so evident in his eyes. "But if you have—uh—a thing for wizards—"

"Oh. Fuck. I'm sorry, man."

Now I feel like twice the asshole for nearly backing out myself.

"I'm sure they know you worked hard to put this all together. It's just probably—you know, bad luck. Poor timing. Alignment of the planets."

"Yeah. I guess," Matt grimaces. "One of my friends got called in to cover a shift at work. Another guy said he forgot about his girlfriend's birthday. And this one guy—apparently he still had a hangover from last night."

"That's one hell of a hangover."

Weak-ass excuses, if we're honest.

Not that I'm much better, assembling this punk rock pornstar get-up just to conquer my social anxiety.

"Yeah, no kidding."

"Well—" I attempt a reassuring smile, "Can *I* come in?"

"*Oh*. Yeah, sorry." He holds the door open for my benefit.

"You apologize too much."

The first thing I notice is the smell.

Cats. He's definitely got cats.

I survey the rest as I unlace.

It's a long procedure. Plenty of time to take in his abandoned roleplay set-up, with its dry-erase map, themed dice sets and tiny, hand-painted figurines.

My gaze continues across the room, taking in his impressive collection of Salvatore and Weis-Hickman paperbacks. The occasional Gonzo anime boxset. He's got fan art posters lovingly mounted in chipped dollar store frames. Comic first editions taped up next to them in their plastic packaging.

Mostly retro horror covers.

Now I know what drew him to my table at that ill-fated craft fair.

My poor inkwork monsters could not have felt more out of place between Monica's Just 4 You organic hand cream and homecrafted candles from One of a Kind Dreamz.

The real question is what he was doing at that kind of event in the first place. I was just desperate for extra pocket change. Whereas Matt—

Maybe he's got a girlfriend.

Fuck me. I should have thought to ask.

A wet nose interrupts my internal train crash.

"His name's Jiji."

I raise a hand for Jiji to sniff. He's an inquisitive black cat, perfect for his namesake. "Like Jiji from Kiki's Delivery Service?"

"Yeah," I detect a note of hesitation in his voice. "My ex named him."

Oh? *Do tell.*

"So he wasn't always your cat?"

Jiji insinuates himself into my arms. I raise him off the ground. Matt is watching me rather intently as I scratch the warm mass of purring black fur between the ears.

"No, he wasn't. My ex used to live here. We got him together, but she moved out a few months ago, so—" He pauses, stifling what appears to be an undertone of bitterness. "Apparently her place isn't exactly pet friendly. I still haven't found anyone to take the new spare bedroom."

They shared a cat and a two-bedroom apartment. This was no weekend Tinder hookup. Is the poor man rebounding so hard he ended up in a whole other hemisphere?

"How long were you together?"

"Three years."

"Huh. That's tough."

"Yeah," Matt looks as though it ages him another three just to acknowledge it.

"Parted on good terms though?"

"Well—sort of, yeah."

"Sort-of?" I raise my eyebrows.

Matt caves. Doesn't take much, it seems. I get the impression he's had little opportunity to discuss the explosion of this relationship outside the confines of ground zero.

"She was going into grad school for social work." His tone is measured. Deliberately aloof, like that of a man describing the inevitable. "I wasn't really getting along with her new friends. She said she felt trapped. That she needed a change. I guess she just wanted to try something new."

Somebody new, you mean. Grad school for social work. New friends. Of course, now it all makes sense.

Why Matt of all people had a passing conversational familiarity with terms like trans and sub, but no first-hand experience. Why he was so remarkably willing to attempt nude modelling for a stranger, and yet a complete bundle of nerves once he actually arrived.

Why Mr. Just Water took any interest at all in an inveterate genderfreak like me.

"Ah."

Jiji licks my outstretched fingers. I meet Matt's eyes head-on.

"Isn't that what you said you wanted? To try something new?"

I have to admit this isn't a fair question.

Not for lack of sympathy, though it could use a little more of that. I do feel for the guy. Three years. What a brutal way to end it. Toss him away like a used condom.

But it's the unspoken implication that I actually regret.

This isn't a question about his past relationship. It's a question about *me*. Making him bear the weight of my insecurities. Revealing weakness. If I'm lucky, maybe he won't catch on.

"Yeah but—" Matt doesn't meet my gaze. He's got this tight-lipped, uncertain smile. His eyes aren't smiling. "Not in the same way."

"I—" And then the guilt comes flooding out. "Look man, I'm sorry. You had this D&D thing all planned out tonight. Everyone bailed. And here I am, barely past the door, reopening fresh wounds with all these questions about your shitty break-up."

He chuckles. Apology accepted.

"Nah, it's fine. I'm glad you came."

His smile warms to match the temperature of those words.

And just like that, I'm hornier than ever.

Is this really all it takes to get me going? Just someone showing me a little kindness?

Maybe my standards could use a facelift.

Or maybe he's just into you. Maybe you don't have to second-guess every moment of sexual tension in case you're somehow being used or manipulated.

I visualize scrunching my internal monologue into a ball and pitching it in the trash.

"Do you—wanna watch something? I know you said you like Perfect Blue. And honestly, just based on that I think you would actually enjoy Eva. People talk it up, but it really *is* that good."

"Eva? Oh, as in Evangelion." I suppose it is about time.

"I've got some Orville's from Metro."

"Do you have chili powder?"

"What, for popcorn?" He raises his eyebrows like I just requested he load my bowl with mustard and raspberry jam.

"Yeah."

"Seriously?"

"Dead serious. *It's good.*"

This may not be the best time to mention I also eat Sriracha on toast. It's too early for him to know the true depths of my taste bud madness.

"You—want butter on it too?" Matt reaches for a glimmer of familiarity in this strange new world.

"Enough that it sticks."

"Alright, gotcha."

He turns into the adjoining kitchen. It's a doorless corner alcove. The sort of map edge that would get you cornered by ghosts in Pac-man.

I wander around the other side, acquainting myself with Matt's exuberant grandma couch.

Jiji scrambles out of my arms as I survey this marvel of bicentennial kitsch.

Man in the kitchen. This cat knows what's up.

Despite appearances, the fake velour is actually rather comfy.

A flatscreen tv stands across from me on an ornate wooden cabinet that almost certainly came from the same furniture set as this couch. Perhaps it once stored a set of fine wedding china, decorated with rustic scenery.

Now the only thing gathering dust inside that cabinet is a plethora of gaming consoles dating back to the age before DRM.

The hum of the microwave marks the passage of time. Kitchen drawers open. Jiji lets out a plaintive yowl. And having come to a decision, I toss my jacket to the ground.

Matt takes his time with the popcorn. Maybe he's actually counting the gap in pop frequency. Measuring butter by the spoonful. Every passing clang feels tailored to strain the patience of my libido.

Finally, he emerges. A wizard bearing two bowls of marathon snackfood.

"Sorry, I had to feed Jiji too. Otherwise he'd never leave me alone..." Matt trails off, gawking in silence.

"I told you. You apologize too much."

"That's my grandma's old couch." He says this as though it's meant to be some kind of rational deterrent.

"Yeah, I figured."

I arch my back, stretch my arms out, and point my toes. One fluid gesture of relaxation, before settling back into my best Martyrdom of Saint Sebastian impression.

Matt may not know many Renaissance paintings, but I think this pose of affected suffering is universal.

He stands there, bowls still in hand. "Why do I feel like I'm supposed to be doing something?"

"I dunno Matt." I give him a facetious smirk. "Should you be? I am getting a little cold."

Watching him stand there, looking uncertain, I'm momentarily eclipsed by my own doubts. Did I misread the situation? Was last week just a total fluke?

Maybe he wants to make a new friend, and I'm twisting his platonic overtures into an excuse for an amateur porn plot.

"I got Kimonos," he offers, "you know, instead of Durex?"

"Oh, thank god. I was starting to worry."

"About—condoms?"

"About whether you're actually attracted to me."

"Yeah, I—" He finally puts the bowls down. I suppose the lack of a coffee table does make the gesture rather awkward. "Of course I'm attracted to you."

"So get your dick wrapper."

He gives me a quick once-over. A swift mental calculation. "I could bring you to the dick wrapper."

"I bet you could."

He's got a head on me, and I'm one-twenty sopping wet. If grandma's couch is some kind of sacred altar, unblemished by memories of packing his palm to rule thirty four, I'm not complaining about having my feet lifted.

Is he into that? I could be into that.

"It's just that the couch is squeaky," he admits, "and really fucking old."

I let him raise me off of it, wrapping my arms around his neck to make the position a little more sustainable. His robe feels like actual linen. Not the scratchy fabric texture of commercial, off-the-rack cosplay, but a rough, tactile weave. It's pleasant against my bare skin.

"Hey Matt—you think you could keep this on?"

"Wow, you weren't kidding. You're *actually* into wizards."

"I mean—if you met a guy who could cast polymorph and incendiary cloud in real life, wouldn't you at least entertain the idea of sleeping with him?"

He laughs—perhaps in agreement?

It occurs to me that I don't even know if Matt has a history of sleeping with men. I might be his first. The word **experiment** wavers tauntingly in my mind.

I smother it in the cool, dry wrinkles of unmade sheets at my back. The feeling of warm hands receding, almost reluctantly, from my body.

He pulls down the pants beneath his costume, and follows them with a pair of faded boxers. There's no hesitation this time. None of that pretense about working up to it. Speed is the philosophy at work here.

I beckon him unto me.

"No, closer. Rest your knees to either side of my shoulders."

"What, like this?"

My hand draws his penis out from a convenient flap where the layers of the robe converge (*O, the wizard's staff had a knob on the end*).

And take him into my mouth before the temptation to make lewd Discworld references overcomes my sex-addled brain.

I want him to hold my head down. Slam the base of his penis against my moistened lips. Plumb the depths of my throat until I gag.

My clit swells from the hot, viscous mess between my legs.

I can practically feel each thrust in the loosening grip of the passage below, like the walls are receding to admit him.

Of course, I know this to be a ploy. They'll clutch and squeeze like a hardened fist the moment he's within their grasp.

"Mmnmmph—"

He pulls out. "Are you okay?"

I gasp, choking a little on the overabundance of spit. It's leaking into my facial hair.

He hasn't heard me moan like that. Hard to tell moans of pain from pleasure with someone you're only just discovering.

"Put it on."

There's a crooning lilt to my voice. If I sound like I'm begging, it's because I am. But certainly not for the condom.

He leans over to dig through the bedside drawer. It's close enough that he doesn't have to change position.

All the better to run my hands along his thighs. Dip my fingers under his balls. Trace the vein running the length of his dick.

He trembles, making a noise of pleasure and mild distress. "I'm trying to get it out."

"Try faster." I murmur, unable to restrain a smile.

"Got it now—you can calm down."

Calm down? Ha.

"Absolutely not."

I raise my legs, hooking them around his knees. My feet slither haltingly up the sides of his body, coming to a resting point on his chest. Loose fibres tease between my toes. Then I slip my hand to my clit. Taunting myself with slow, kneading fingers.

"Kneel in, like you're folding me double."

The crook of each knee rises to his shoulders as he lowers himself against me. Into me. I love the way his body fills the space between us. I want to be filled. Flattened into the bed. I want to feel enveloped so completely, I can hardly breathe.

I'd tell him to go harder now, but my voice is lost in a series of deep, shuddering gasps.

The thrusting of his body against mine feels like one continuous wave. A current rising and receding. I'm caught up in it. The slippery head of my clit brushing repeatedly against his torso.

A throbbing pulse—submerging me, even without the help of fingers.

I cling to him, inside and out. Let my convulsions do the talking. Go on. Fill me all the way. I want you so deep I lose sight of everything.

Broken syllables echo in my head. A steady, rhythmic pulse of words.

Just the wet smack of his balls and the soft creak of the bed frame. The tremor in his breathing. The low groan. Or was that my own voice? I love it when I can't tell.

Do I want to come like this?

"M-matt—"

"Yeah?"

He sounds so close, yet eons away. I have to press up against his chest, fighting to summon enough air into my lungs for more than a one-word stutter.

"Turn me over. I want to feel you deeper."

I consider switching to anal. Letting him strike the back of my clit as I stroke the swollen front. I know I'm good for it.

But then I consider his relative inexperience. Weigh the negotiation of possibilities- the inevitable butt talk- against my fleeting whims, and think better of it.

Let's keep it simple.

I conspire with his arms to flip my body over on its front. It makes me feel lithe. Small and agile, with his hands bracing my lean hips. I can feel myself instinctively sticking my ass out. Squirming playfully in his grasp.

"Hmph—" That was definitely the beginning of a laugh.

I may not see his face, but I can feel him smiling. Feel his hands tracing the treasure trail running between my ribs, down the slight incline of my belly. All the way down. Stroking my clit. I wince at the sudden thrill of his touch.

"H-how does it feel?"

The laughter is in his voice too. "Shouldn't I be asking you that?"

"I mean-" How can I explain it?

It's the most genderfucked part of my body. This tent of engorged tissue, rising over the folds of my labia. Not quite large enough to stroke with a full hand, but too thick and protruding for the flick of fingers when it swells.

Am I asking if it unsettles him? This peculiar amalgamation of parts that doesn't map onto any medical textbook or highschool health class- does he- like it?

"Am I doing this right?" He sounds tentative. Genuinely concerned.

"Yeah, you can—" **Oh. Oh fuck.** My hips gyrate in tandem with his fingers. "You can, uh—pull a little harder."

"Aughgkhkh—" I can barely stop myself from snapping my legs together. Whatever-that-sound-was ends in a plaintive wail.

"Sounds like I'm doing something right."

"Y-yeah-ha-ha—" I try to pull myself together long enough to produce coherent language, "Think you can do that while you fuck me?"

"I think so."

I moan as he enters me.

Any remaining appearance of sobriety dissipates like cold sweat. Again and again, like an out-of-tune guitar. Pluck my strings until you've found your chord.

It's hard holding that position. My arms are a bracket against his momentum, threatening to bury me in his bed.

I sense that he wants to up the tempo, whether he knows it or not. Mounting urgency. Escalating in bursts. I take over for his hand.

Bend forward until my chest is riding every squeal of the mattress. Give him free reign to pound me into the pillows.

My insides throttle his firm shaft. Feel the immensity of each thrust. Just fucking impale me.

Tear me wide open. The pillow runs wet with my sweltering breath. My plucked strings. Go on and smash that guitar. **Destroy me.**

Thick. Hot. Hard. Breathe. Warm. Fuck.

I somehow howl and sob and cry out.

White noise. *Static.*

Did he say something?

Too often I have to lure myself into it. Seduce my brain into compliance with the right thoughts. The proper gestures.

But this feels organic. Like he gave it to me. This deluge of sheer bliss is *his fault.*

I realize my knees have collapsed onto the bed.

His unfettered pounding feels brutally good. I'm riding the verge of a second orgasm. But I doubt he'll last that long.

Not with my insides gripping him for dear life, throbbing in the aftershock of my climax, and my back flush against his body. Flesh viciously entwined. A perfect fit.

He whimpers deep into my neck. I feel him come. A heightened pulse. A series of short, desperate palpitations. Nails digging into skin. Succumbing to rapture and exhaustion.

He's really sweating through all that linen.

I'm raw. Rubbed sore. Loving every spasm.

We both pant like overheated dogs.

Finally, Matt rolls onto his back. "Wow. You like it hard, huh?"

I take my first deep breath in what seems like eternity.

"Sometimes you just wanna bang," *But not always.* My lips curl into a teasing smile. "Thanks for all your hard work."

"No problem." He grins. "Uh, I'll be right back—"

He's off the bed with surprising swiftness.

I watch the robe recede from sight, hoping he'll take it off, now that the novelty has faded. It seems I have a hunger for skin that linen just can't satisfy.

Then my attention drifts, noting the blackout curtains at the window. Sure sign of a night shift worker. Piles of clothing on the floor. Mismatched socks among the bed sheets. I realize, with a flood of appreciation, that he's got a lampshade printed with the deliciously vintage faces of early 20th-century horror.

I feel his weight distend the mattress, and look up.

"Still good for watching Eva, by the way. If you are." I try to match that with a reassuringly casual smile. *Don't worry, I'm not catching emotions. Who's catching emotions? Not me.*

But he's already surprisingly close. Looming over me. Pleasantly free of linen. "Can we just—stay here for a bit?"

"Tired?" My tone is mellow. I hope it doesn't sound chiding. I was actually pretty impressed by his stamina.

He drops down next to me. "Don't like cuddling?"

Oh. I see.

"I *can* like cuddling."

I turn. He draws me in and kisses me.

My little gothic heart *skips* a beat.

"Maybe we can watch it later tonight? Unless you've got somewhere else to be?" He looks genuinely worried about those hypothetical *other places.*

"Nowhere else I'd *rather* be."

Matt smiles in the awkwardly sweet way of someone who doesn't know how to take a compliment. It's a very familiar expression. I make it all the time.

"Can I ask you something?"

"Yeah?"

"What are you looking for exactly? I mean, you just got out of a three year relationship—what— several months ago?"

I recognize his twinge of discomfort. But there's too much in the way of tender gestures and affectionate glances making their rounds here not to, at the very least, broach the question.

So I keep pushing. "Do you want something casual? A fuckbuddy? FWB?"

Do you just want to assuage the loneliness? "Not that I don't empathize. But if you need to fill a girlfriend-shaped gap, and that means grasping at anything within reach, I have to know."

And just like that, I know we're about to have *the conversation*.

"You're direct."

"I get that a lot."

"No, direct is good. My ex was very passive-aggressive so—" He trails off. Realizing, I assume, that this doesn't answer the question.

"I guess—you know, we met and—I thought you seemed pretty cool. It's still kind of hard to believe that you're into me, to be honest but—" He chuckles in mild embarrassment. "I thought maybe we'll just hang out. See where it goes."

"Are you bisexual?" Damn, Alex. Really hammering those nails in today.

"I—guess so? I haven't really dated a lot of people."

"You don't have to date people to know for sure."

What I'm really asking is—

But I can see the substance of the question finally clicks with him. I want to know if he's using me as a stepping stone to figure out his sexuality. A kind of safe, murky in-between while he summons the bravery to admit his attraction to cisgender men.

"There was this guy, Kenneth. We met at Anime North. This was before Dana, my ex. I think he—might've been a furry? We did this online thing. It's weird. He seemed more into talking about sex than actually doing it."

"Yeah, I think I know the type."

"Anyway, we hung out maybe a couple of times in person and then he sort of ghosted me. I'd tried watching gay porn before, but I guess I felt like I wouldn't really know until I tried it. And I'm not really into the club scene? Grindr just freaks me out."

"The plight of queer nerds everywhere," I chuckle to myself.

Alright, question sufficiently answered.

"Seriously." Matt looks like he's barely restraining a flood of questions himself. "How about you?"

"Well, before my transition, I dated women pretty much exclusively. Thought I had that whole SuicideGirl tomboy-femme thing worked out."

I can read that look in his eyes. The one people give me when they're imagining my past self, projected onto my current body.

"Oh yeah?" But he's giving me the floor. Enough room for more than the tired trans origin story box step routine.

"Thing is, I'd never let them touch me. Had a *Stone Butch Blues* approach before I'd ever heard of Leslie Feinberg. I could handle gendered bullshit from strangers, but the mere thought of being seen as a woman in any intimate setting—of living, trapped in that foreign chassis for life—that was some real body horror shit."

"So—"

I laugh, precluding the implication. "Yeah, I've been with all sorts of people since I began my transition."

And in case he also wants unambiguous reassurance—

"Eight years of HRT and a bilateral mastectomy later is enough time to suck my fair share of cisgender dick."

"But did you always know?"

"What, that I was bi? Trans?"

"Yeah." He looks as though he's afraid of offending me.

Fortunately for Matt, I'm one thick-skinned queer.

"Well, I didn't always have the vocabulary. Or the self-respect to live honestly. I even tried to make the woman thing work, but in the end—"

I look down at myself. Small, bony, unshaven Alex.

"This is the only body that fit."

Please don't say you think I'm brave.

"It does seem like a pretty good one."

"Thanks. *Custom-made.*" And just like that, in this moment, with this man, everything's fine. I almost feel safe here.

I could get used to this. If I allowed it.

"Alex?"

"Hm?" I rest my head below his chest, absentmindedly tracing the shape of his nipples with my fingers.

"You still wanna watch Eva?" He looks a little embarrassed, as though his question betrays a lack of social skills.

All it tells me is I'm not the only one who could use a brain-scrubbing. After sinking our minds deep in that insecurity quagmire, any distraction would be a blessing.

"Sure. But I'm not putting my pants back on."

"Fine by me." I feel his hand finding its way to my ass.

"Fuck, Matt. You know I have no refractory period, right? Are you *trying* to get me going?"

He laughs. *Buddy, you think I'm joking?* I wonder if he's feeling the very real floodgates lifting between my legs.

"Guess I'll have to be more careful."

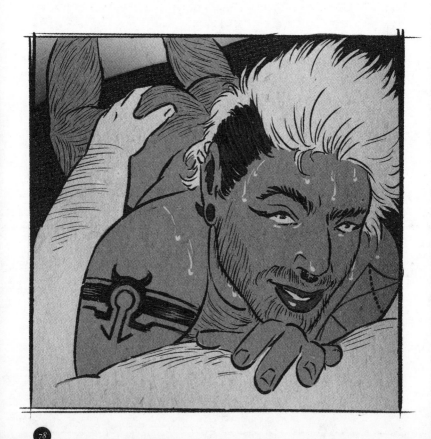

How will We Be Replenished?

"Who will love us,"
We ask ourselves,
"If we cannot learn
To love ourselves."
Who taught us that love
comes from nothing?
That it is
An inexhaustible source.
That it is
A force of indomitable strength.
We have seen our love parched,
starved and gasping for air.
Who will love us?

Part III

Dedicated to those of us who were

taught to feel monstrous

FOR DARING TO EXIST.

We who are barely a footnote

in biology,

but an entire genre

of pornography.

Who watch as mothers

clutch their children tighter

when we pass them on the street.

Who read the faces

of affably forward strangers

like an omen of death.

Our presence in their world is

Degenerate.

Unhinged.

Political.

BUT IT IS OUR WORLD TOO.

Rain patters against my basement window. The autumn chill has finally seeped through the cracks.

I rest a hot mug on the blanket covering my chest. It's just that stinging bit too hot. Startling me from a slow, silent film reel of insecurities. I'm awaiting his message more eagerly than I

care to admit.

I've been thinking of you.

> Hey.

I often wonder what you're up to between our nightly texting marathons.

> What's up?

I often question your feelings for me.

Interrogating your phrasing and choice of words. Searching for hidden admissions of care, even as I painstakingly scrub my messages clean of any feeling at all.

> You got something for me yet?

Seen. Three dots. An animated ellipsis.

I swallow down a smile that feels embarrassingly wide. Let my thoughts sink into the comfort of warm, itchy wool and rising steam.

The buzz of the phone reaches me before I can sink too deep.

I flick open his message link, eager for the next installment in our unspoken challenge.

Tentacles.

My screen is overtaken by them.

An animated body suspended amidst damp, quivering appendages. Squirming their way into every orifice, phallus-shaped protrusions thrust themselves from an impossibly small, spit-streaked mouth.

I think the artist's intention was to make it seem as though their character was penetrated clean through. Like the human body is no skeleton wreathed in fat and muscle, but rather a vessel of pleasure. An elastic plaything.

I can't help but smirk. *Weak, Matt.* That shit's *weak.* Everybody and their conservative uncle has secretly watched tentacle porn by this point.

Meh.

Send me the **real trash**, you coward. The .gif file that made you recoil from your laptop in horror once the orgasmic haze had faded.

I back up my words with an image from my personal collection of oddities.

Anthropomorphic monsters with massive cocks and human breeding farms. Shrinking men and their towering, ravenous lovers. Bondage toeing a dangerous line with the consensual pretense of non-consent.

And that's just scratching the surface of the internet.

Dislocated from reality and safely controlled, we can turn any horror into a fuckfest. And then we have the gall to wash our hands, vow to keep our lips forever sealed, and treat this feat of imagination like it's something unclean.

Sometime, some place, something's got to give. The conscious personality must integrate the shadow. *Thanks, Carl Jung.*

My screen glows against the backdrop of a crack of thunder.

> **Wow ok**

> **Clearly I wasn't taking this contest seriously enough**

> **Hope you're ready**

I settle back into the couch. My tea has grown ferociously bitter. The last sip strips my gums dry. But even that can't break my cheshire cat grin.

It takes several agonizing minutes to load.

His file must be megabytes deep. A scrambled, unreadable name, as enigmatic as the unmarked bag concealing a back massager from the local Stag Shop.

I steel myself for any number of wildly unsettling fetishes. Something as likely to trigger my gag reflex as to bring on the bedroom eyes.

Then I tap the download link.

My mouth forms the wordless shape of surprise, closely followed by a firm line of irritation.

It's a beautiful image. I'll give it that. Bed sheets split by the shadow of leafy branches from a nearby window. The amber palette of a sunrise. Hair and hands intermingling. A painted couple spoons amid the pillows, partially concealed by a quilted comforter.

Are you trying to tell me something, Matt?

Go on then. Get it over with.

Way to subvert the rules.

There were rules? ;)

You know what you did.

The animated ellipses flicker and reappear. A message written, rethought, and attempted again.

Can I ask you a question?

k

A single, wary letter to match the way I feel about his question.

There is another pause. Thoughts cautiously parceled into words. I can almost see his thumb wavering over the send button.

Are you scared of intimacy or is it just that you don't want that kind of relationship with me?

All remnants of a smile drop off my face.

I flick my screen back to the download. His latest submission to our contest, and likely the one to prematurely end it.

So the man has a sense of humour.

I put my phone down, leave the mug on the floor, and flop my head back. The never-ending rain knocks against my window more insistently than ever. Shadows of the ceiling fan flicker above me. I can hear its mechanical thrum.

The gears in my brain are turning. My discarded phone punctuates the slow, steady ambiance of my soundscape. Once. Then again. Then several more times. Practically setting a rhythm of its own.

Is he writing a thesis in that chatbox? *"Treatise on the not-so-hidden fears of Alex Mazor"?* God help me.

With one stiff, long-suffering motion, I raise myself back to a sitting position.

My gaze settles on the phone like a house centipede spotted across the room. I'm giving it the same distrustful look. Considering my options with the same reluctant urgency.

Finally, I pick it up again. I'm bracing myself, much as I did for the egregious smut that never came.

I read his newest message first.

> **I'm still driving you tonight either way. So don't worryy**

> **Noted.**

About time to get ready, isn't it?

I make my way to the closet, absorbing the rest of his messages as I go.

There's an anxious warmth to it all. A rambling confession that has very little to do with me.

My left hand picks through lace straps and faux leather as the other finds the beginning of his monologue and scrolls down.

Even the start is messy.

The kind of typo-ridden rush job you'd expect from your freshman roommate at 4 am, after dropping that last tear-ridden phone call from their (ex) high school sweetheart.

But we're old enough to have happily married friends. He doesn't want to burden them

with the absence of his ex. It's lonely, he types, having a bed entirely to himself for the first time in years.

I pick out a shimmering black mass. The sequined top that might as well be scaled, and glossy vinyl too skimpy and skintight to rightfully be described as pants.

My finger pauses on the part about hobbies and obsessions that don't seem as fulfilling when indulged alone. He describes fear of connection. And the crippling desire for it.

I find a tube of lipstick lurking in my bathroom drawer, nestled between my box of injection needles and a near-empty vial of depo-testosterone. It's a rich, sultry maroon.

Might as well go full homme fatale.

The last dregs of his rambling confession are about *us*.

If the way he feels in the aftermath of his break-up is too much, Matt wants me to know he'll understand. It's alright if I think he's clingy. He won't hold it against me if I end it here, knowing he needs affection like a fix.

I brush the loose hair from my face, tightening my braid to match the growing tightness at the base of my throat.

My choices feel cowardly now.

The cultivated distance. Keeping him in the proverbial waiting room. Number in hand, but no receptionist in sight.

Can't I show a little vulnerability? Even a glimpse?

I envision a suitable apology, posed behind my own front door like something midway between a Golden Age of Hollywood diva and a trapdoor spider.

I practice radiating desire.

My bags stand fully packed to either side.

I look down at the phone again. Scroll and scroll. Twitter feeds and emails. Rage-filled news articles. Make-up tutorials. Ads for things I'll never buy that clearly got lost somewhere in the muddled algorithm of my Google consumer personality.

Anything at all to put off responding to his messages with something of substance.

Finally he knocks.

My phone screen lights up, making me realize that I've been waiting in utter darkness.

Yes, I can tell.

I open the door and start dragging the suitcase past him before he can offer. "There's another bag in there."

"Sure." And he's on it.

One of those guys, I think to myself. The world is divided between men who jump at the opportunity to carry heavy objects, and those who watch, helpless to stop them.

I brush past him in the narrow hallway to lock the door. My hand remains firm on the one thing I *am* holding. I don't even know when I acquired the habit of insisting the carrying types won't take them all. Fortunately for him, he doesn't ask.

"Well?" Matt smiles in a high-strung sort of way.

I nod. "Yep, let's go."

"You look good."

I glance at him out of the corner of my eye. His tone leaves me with the feeling that he was saving that one. It was supposed to be his greeting.

My smile tightens. I've only just realized I was smiling at all. "Yeah? Not…*different?*"

"I could get used to it," Matt says. The mischievous expression lingers even as he finishes his thought.

"Cool. You look good too."

I can read the anxiety in his restless motions. The questions he so desperately wants to ask.

For the few minutes it takes him to Tetris his way around the loaded trunk, I actively consider taking the back seat. It feels like the decision between making him my voluntary chauffeur or...*something else*. Under the front door overhang, just out of reach of the rain, my thoughts are as murky as the sodden footpath drenching my heels in mud.

I think better of it. No reason to define *something else* just yet.

There's a graveyard of drive-through boxes in the front seat, but I clear them out before he can start apologizing.

"Oh, sorry, let me get those—" Matt materializes on the other side, with his hand outstretched. So much for skipping the mandatory apology.

"It's fine."

So now we've both made it into the car. Successfully, without saying a word about those messages. Matt starts the engine. I struggle a little too long with the seatbelt. By the time I look up again, we're already on the road.

"Excited about the show?" Matt tries, testing the waters.

"Well, I've only got the one piece in it. It's nice for publicity. But the artists' market tomorrow is the real reason I'm going. This opening exhibition is just a glorified peer-to-peer networking event."

Now that I've admitted it aloud, my stomach drops for all sorts of reasons unrelated to the conversation we *aren't* having.

Networking events bring out my inner misanthrope. I'm already awkward, and we aren't even in the room yet.

"But it's still something, right?" Matt insists, in that adorable way of someone who was taught artists are supposed to be in galleries.

I indulge the need to look at him again. He really does look good. Hell, the man cleans up better than I do.

That smartly folded collar framing a well-trimmed beard is perfect. And the queer in me loves that he chose to wear a bowtie. Upon closer inspection, I notice its patterned green and black squares are actually oversized 8-bit space invaders. *Never change, Matt.*

His suit is a close fit. It's flattering. Doesn't read like a rental.

I muzzle the temptation to make a sarcastic remark about whether he last wore it to prom night. The fact that he made an effort makes me nervous. Nothing brings out my sass like unease.

Finally, I manage to respond. "I'm just glad to have some backup."

And some perverse instinct in me has already placed a manicured hand on his thigh before I finish the sentence.

"Please. Don't do that. I'm driving."

I've never heard a man sound giddier about saying no.

Wordlessly, I retract the gesture. But I'm smiling. We both are.

His shoulders look broad and capable in their posture at the wheel. He's tamed his curls with some kind of scentless pomade. There's an air of resolve about this get-up that I haven't seen on him before.

I realize it's not unlike my own.

Armour to disguise our vulnerabilities.

We're not going to resolve this here, on this treacherous road in the midst of rain and city traffic. Not if we want to survive the trip to Hamilton.

I nearly fall asleep.

It's the internal rhythms of the vehicle. The start and stop, jostling me back and forth, constant drizzle and click of the windshield wipers. The overactive heating. And our silence, all melding together into one of those aimless, fragmented dreams you only remember when waking.

"Hey Alex?"

It startles me to hear him say my name. There are days when I'm still floored by anyone using the correct name at all. But something about hearing it spoken so naturally by the man I fucked sends adrenaline coursing through my blood.

I blink several times. Then all at once my mascara-laden eyelashes snap wide open, and I'm as prepared as I'll ever be.

"Right, yeah."

We're parked in the motel driveway. The rain has lifted, replaced by a bleak humidity that makes every breath feel more laboured than the last. I'm emboldened by the rare breeze.

Matt's presence makes clearing up room bookings with exhausted strangers feel much easier. Even when it comes to explaining the mismatch in my ID.

We find ourselves with two beds. I confess I don't remember asking. Perhaps it's just the nature of their rooms. Washed-out linens and a grey, featureless carpet. When it comes to events like this, I'm so tired by the end of the night that I hardly notice.

But I never negotiated that premise with Matt.

I told him the bus route was a pain. He offered to drive. He offered to stay and drive me back. I pay for our room and gas. That was our whole arrangement, and not a word more.

In the weeks leading up to the artists' market I was so busy drawing, writing, printing— endlessly producing for hours on end.

I never even gave it a second thought.

Now that we're here, I have countless worries about how this weekend will unfold.

My eyes follow his reflection in the cabinet mirror. Conveniently placed across from the two beds, it perfectly encapsulates the opposite end of the room. I'm pretending to correct my make-up. He's unpacking some clothing and junk food.

"I've got one free guest pass," I admit. "You're on the list if you want to come."

He looks startled, "I didn't know you needed a pass."

I grin, in spite of myself. "And here I thought you got all dressed up to play at being my personal driver."

Matt approaches from behind me. There's a disconcerted, lumbering manner to his steps that instantly makes me feel bad for teasing him. "You do know I came to see your artwork at the show, right? Like, I don't have anything against Hamilton…"

"Oh, come on. You can admit it. Everyone's got something against Hamilton."

He chuckles. "Well, nobody leaves Toronto for the weekend to party it up in Hamilton, that's for sure."

"Yeah. I know. I just wasn't sure this would be your thing."

I wince a little as my meticulously painted cat eye nearly smudges into my hairline. The excuse of correcting my face is wearing thin. Another moment of pretense, and I might just ruin it.

"Hey, I met you at an artists' market, remember?"

"Were you there for the *art?*" I look up, genuinely curious.

He clicks his tongue, in the way of someone caught in a small lie.

"Yeeah, well—*not exactly*. There was this guy selling custom dice sets outside, and I was having kind of a shit day. So I thought, what the hell. Why not check it out?"

I smile at my memory of Matt as the quiet, fumbling customer.

He lingered on the periphery of my wavering tide of onlookers. The type who clearly had a lot to say, but didn't want to bother the artist with his questions.

I've developed a mercantile instinct for his type of bystander. Engage them with one of several well-practiced lines. They're usually too polite to refuse.

"So you think you can handle a whole weekend of the stuff? Maybe even see what it's like in the booth?"

"Sure, I'll earn my keep." He grins. A little too enthusiastically, I think. Eight straight hours of exhibition crowds will rob him of that fervour.

But I'm grateful for the banter. The sense of new normal that we're establishing between us.

Matt leans in. "Are you ready? It's almost nine."

"Damn. Nine already?" I glance towards the obligatory glass sliding door leading into the parking lot. "How is it *this dark* at nine?"

My stiletto heels come away from the street mired in wet gravel. Our motel is only a ten-minute sprint from the convention centre, and I insist on walking when I can.

From the moment we acquire our name tags and wine tickets at the front desk, I know Matt's presence will be a saving grace.

Everywhere I look, I see women in fitted cocktail dresses with artless boyfriends in identical suits, dangling like accessories on their arms.

All deeply gender-normative. Engaged in polite conversations about mortgages and vacations. Mostly white.

Abstract paintings and portrait photography dominate the room. There are plaques on every wall, explaining their profound significance. We pass metallic installations that would make very boring playgrounds. Video reels cutting personal webcam footage with chase sequences from American cartoons.

I'm steering through the crowd with a dogged single-mindedness. Matt seems to catch on.

He gestures, "There's the bar."

We locate my painting with drinks in hand. It's a wall piece. Eighteen by thirty-two. My first in a *very long time*.

A misshapen nightmare-being poses at the edge of a bare mattress. It forms seductive gestures with its multitude of emaciated arms.

Its eyes are milky-white. No pupils. A thinning blanket is drawn over its contorted form in something like a failed attempt at modesty.

The creature smiles, almost pathetically. There is a certain charm in its terrifying features and amorous overtures.

Or maybe that's just how I see it now, months later. Long since separated from the sleepless nights that brought it into this world.

My last living brain cell is wrestling with the thought that Matt might misread my inspiration. Will he notice the similarity in its pose, and take this as some kind of insult? Or will he see it for what it is—the projection of my inner demons on the living canvas of another. A person as whole and as fractured as myself.

It's more of an apology than anything.

"Wow," Matt offers appreciatively, "that's fucked up."

"Yeah, no kidding." I start to laugh in relief. *Inner demons are like that.*

"It's wild though. Like it really gets to you. I'm seeing this in my nightmares for sure."

"You better. I worked my ass off on that thing."

"You're good at this, you know." He sounds earnest.

"Thanks but—" I glance back towards the crowd. My face has adopted a perpetual smirk. Probably since the moment I walked in. "This shit right here, it's lowbrow."

Matt's face suggests he's about to protest, so I qualify the word.

"This isn't exactly the meeting ground for horror artists who moonlight in indie book covers."

"Oh. Yeah," Matt says, gazing around with one hand in his pocket, and the other on his empty glass, "I think I'm starting to see that."

"Frankly, I still can't believe they featured it at all. Exhibitor spots are one thing. We pay for those. But this—" I shrug. "I guess somebody on the judges' panel discovered they had an imagination."

Matt looks up at the painting again. There's a curiosity in his gaze. As though he's not merely looking, but *seeing* it. Quietly, he assures me, "We can leave any time you like."

I'm about to suggest the time is now, when I notice we aren't my creature's sole audience.

There's a small group of women assembling behind us. They seem to be making their way across the hall.

"Oh. That's *ghastly*. I don't like that at all."

Matt casts a sly sideways glance in my direction. I smile at him. Of course I have the artist's compulsion to remain when there are vocal spectators to be had.

If they're revolted, I want to hear about it.

"It's just—you know, it's so *creepy*. I don't want to know what kind of person would think to paint something like that."

"I just think they should have a warning. Maybe put it behind a curtain? It could make somebody *very* uncomfortable."

I nudge Matt. "They should put us behind a curtain. You know, with a content warning."

Matt nods very seriously. "Some people might get uncomfortable."

Just as I think we managed our brief exchange out of earshot, and the company of politely offended women has fled our corrupting presence—I notice someone drawing nearer.

I'm awful at recognizing faces. My brain treats any information collected in a crowd of strangers like rainwater in a drainage ditch. So I can't tell if this woman was with the group. I can't even tell how long she was lurking in our vicinity before she got much too close for comfort.

"Is this your work?" She breaks into an indulgent smile. "Do you mind if I ask you a question?"

"Go right ahead." I'm already beginning to catalogue a mental list of inspirations. Favourite artists. Entertaining stories of nights spent toiling over coffee cups that were easily confused with water thickened by paint. Maybe I could tell her about the time—

"What are your pronouns?"

Oh. I wonder who taught her that question.

"He." I smile thinly, "Just he."

"Oh, okay." Something about her expression suggests this isn't what she expected to hear. Or perhaps it's just my discomfort projected onto her momentary silence. I will myself not to think too deeply on it.

"Your make-up is very nice."

"Thanks."

But she lingers, as though there's something left unsaid. I'm starting to dread every next word.

When she leans in, she doesn't lower her voice. "You are so brave. And don't let anyone tell you otherwise, okay? *You are as much a woman as any woman here.*"

Oh god.

"Actually, uh, I'm not…"

"He's a dude," Matt confirms from behind me, "a dude who wears make-up. It's not that complicated."

The woman, who has clearly only just noticed him, shoots Matt a look that could assassinate unsuspecting Starbucks baristas for miles. "Excuse me. *He* is a *she.*"

"Matt, *it's fine.* She thinks I transitioned in the opposite direction."

It happens so often in these pseudo-profound contemporary arts environments, with their audience of self-congratulatory allies, I wonder at myself for not summoning a better comeback.

She's expecting easy tells. My visible gender variance—the sequins and beard, lipstick and effeminate male voice—these are her mental caricature of a trans woman. A trans man, if she can even imagine one, looks like a plaid-shirted tomboy, complete with quiff hairstyle and awkward swagger. And in her misplaced righteous rage, she won't hear otherwise. Certainly not from *me*.

"Yeah, I get it." Matt stares evenly back at her with the perfected indifference of a man who's seen everything there is to see behind a counter working the cash register.

"Let's go."

As I take Matt's arm, I consider how I thought this evening would unravel. How I envisioned his discomfort at the proximity to my obvious genderfuckery in this crowded room.

I was so prepared to watch him distance himself for fear of what others might think of him. *You fucked what?* ***That thing?***

Or worse, paint himself as some kind of hero for deigning to fuck me at all. ***So brave!*** Cashing out in the sexual economy of woke points! Crossing the carnival sideshow off his list!

I hate feeling grateful for his composure.

"Where are we going?" Matt looks patient, but concerned.

We're at the top of the stairs, already well out of the exhibition hall.

It's dark up here. A hallway of mysterious shuttered doors, preceding a railing looking down at the ground floor, and the glass walls above. You can see passing cars, but the sounds are decidedly that of polite laughter and aggressively upbeat music from below.

I find myself longing for the rumble of engines and brisk evening air instead.

"Are you okay?"

"I'm fine." I'll face it again tomorrow.

Tomorrow, there's actually a profit margin.

I'm at the railing, leaning over it. Something about the glass walls and hanging too far over the edge feels like freefall. Like the rush of succumbing to gravity.

"Hey, you wanna know something funny?"

Matt indulges the impulse, joining me at the railing. "What?"

"I never thought this would happen to me but—you know, I used to hang with all these guys who'd joke about the accidental hard-ons they got when the teacher called them to the board in math class."

"Yeah?" He smiles awkwardly.

"What, you too?"

"I mean, not like that exactly—"

"Well people don't talk the same way about so-called *girl parts*. But at some point I realized that I also get boners when I'm anxious. It's just my clit is a whole inch long. So I only *feel* like everyone sees it."

He glances away, laughing silently. "That *is* funny. I think most guys worry about anxiety killing their erection. Not the other way around."

"Yeah, but then there's the whole thing about cortisol kicking your libido into hyperdrive. Stress is weird. It goes both ways."

I give him a significant look.

The proverbial *read-between-the-lines*. And he is. I can see his thoughts churning up a storm behind that placid expression.

"Did you—see my texts?" He meets my gaze.

Fuck. Well, I knew this was coming.

I would have to address it eventually.

"I like you, Matt."

"But?" He chuckles.

That's the sound of a man prepared for averting emotional catastrophe. As though manufactured indifference is any substitute for the real thing.

"I'm scared."

I say it as matter-of-factly as I can. And we see each other.

For one long moment, that's all we do.

Cis men scare the fuck out of me. It's true. I hate it, but there it is. He's afraid of a broken heart and I'm afraid of another garnish of bruises out of sight of prying eyes.

No—that's *not* true.

Not the bruises. *The indignity.* The knowledge of being *less-than.* We're the same species until we suddenly *aren't.*

I could care less about the bruises. The ones I've known have long since faded.

I have thick skin. I do. But I want you to *see me.*

Matt leans closer. I appreciate that he doesn't ask *what* I'm scared of.

Damn right, I'm scared. Who isn't? He's scared too. Maybe of me. Maybe a little of himself.

"Okay," he whispers.

My fingers are in his beard. It's coarse, but softer than my untreated stubble. I can imagine that texture in all sorts of places.

I lock lips with him. My kisses are insistent. I coax his tongue into my mouth. It feels like a welcome penetration. I want it deeper.

He reaches for my waist. My ass. My thighs. The sequins are like snakeskin.

What else can you do with your tongue, Matt?

I push back against him, hoisting myself onto the railing. It's just thick enough. But I'm short. My legs waver in the air. I feel like a gymnast, with my arms on the balance beam. The top lifts. And all I've got is backless PVC leggings. My briefs are well and soaked.

"They're practically fused to my clit and nobody can see a thing. Lucky me, huh?"

Matt laughs.

I could attempt some justification. Tell him that I hate crotch sweat, and the opening in my would-be leggings is just a matter of personal comfort. But who am I kidding? I know it's easy access.

"Don't fall, okay?" He wraps his arms around my waist like he's holding me up.

We both know my arms are doing all the work. I let him hold me anyway. I want to feel his warm body pressed against me. I want to feel the erection his clothing can't hide.

Matt kisses me again. But I'm impatient now. The incursions of his tongue are starting to feel like teasing.

"Hey," –I pull away– "my other lips could use some love too."

"You know this is like—a public place, right?" He raises his eyebrows like he means it. But I sense he's making the point because he feels he must. *Somebody must think of the children!* Or more precisely, the busybodies who will.

"Nothing like a blowjob hidden in plain sight."

"Okay, but if somebody calls the cops or something—"

"Matt, you're a white guy in a fancy suit. Nobody's coming to arrest you for eating me out on an indoor balcony."

I say that as though I'm sure.

Why tell him about the time when some concerned passersby spotted me topless with a middle-aged white guy in a public park?

The way they glared at him as they demanded my ID. The way they looked at me. Pitiable. A victim. *Less-than.* Before they confirmed I was of age.

After that, I was just a whore. *Put a shirt on. Get out of here. Get a fucking room.*

"Show a little backbone, Matt. Go on. *Fuck me up.*"

I spread my legs wide open.

You know Matt? I hate it when they call me brave. I hate it when they call you brave for fucking me. But we *are* brave.

Just not in the way they think.

I run my hands through his curly hair. My fingers curl around his head. *So warm.* He kisses my crotch. It feels like worship. *Pray to your false god, Matt.* I'm so wet, I can hardly feel the texture of your tongue down there.

I moan. My hands tighten on the railing.

Better not slip, Alex.

You're on the edge.

The pressure of his tongue on my clit comes in waves.

So wet it's slick, messy, and gloriously loud. The sound of drops from a faucet that won't close. The sound of tires racing through puddles on a rainy night. The squelch of cheap, waterlogged boots in a storm.

I will myself to keep my legs apart. The big V. What the old pole dancer in me calls *Hello boys.*

He sucks at my clit, and I almost snap them back together.

This is pleasure and pain in a mixing vat. Too intense to stifle my own voice. I want him to stop. I want him to *never* stop.

My pubic hairs mingle with his beard, chafing the all-too-sensitive nerve endings without mercy.

Tickle me raw. Good. *Keep it up.*

And I can hear my own voice. So unlike me, I think. It sounds like surrender. A part of me I hardly know has taken over, and it's having a *great time.*

Then it sounds, all at once, *a little too loud.* Like my phone lighting up in a dark room.

I see faces at the top of the stairs. Looking for the bathroom, I think. A wonder I can think so clearly at all.

Some perverse instinct entices me to moan louder.

I *do* recognize the woman this time.

I hope she recognizes me.

We lock eyes. She's staring in disbelief.

I want her to take in my sequins. My stubble. The voice and the full, painted lips. *Look again, lady. What do you see?*

"Oh my god."

She says it so brusquely. I can hear the noxious mixture of disgust and fascination in her voice. My body shudders with the thrill of our mutual depravity.

Matt stops.

"Bathroom's that way." I point towards a nearby door.

The sign on the door is massive. I hardly need to bother. But it gives me such pleasure to direct her in this moment for which she has no script at all.

I want to see *her* in freefall. *Improvise, lady.*

She click-clacks her way to the bathroom with her shame-faced friend. They're both so comically fixated on looking away, I can barely hold back a laugh.

My eyes follow them all the way to the door.

Matt rests his head against my inner thigh. He's not going to pretend we were doing anything other than the obvious. But neither can he bring himself to continue. *Not here.*

"Hey, you wanna leave now?" I give him a knowing smirk.

Matt pauses before responding. He's brushing some of our coagulated fluids out of his beard.

"Yeaah. I think I'm all art galleried out."

We make our way back to the motel in a way that feels a little too familiar. My fingers are entwined in his, and I'm leaning too close, as though my body is magnetized to his shoulder.

This is a scene in a sad French musical before the lover goes to war. We should have a soundtrack. The rain should fall again, but harder, so it can drench us completely. Quivering with wet and cold, we should leap into each other's arms the moment we shut the door. Full-on movie sex. Heavy breathing and rapid, hungry pawing. Ravenous beasts. The real deal.

"What are you thinking?" He squeezes my hand.

"You think you can finish what you started?"

"Is that it?" He laughs. "You looked really deep in thought."

"*I'm happy.* This is what my *happy* looks like, asshole." I can't keep a straight face. I'm laughing before I even realize it.

"Oh." His self-satisfied sarcasm is a perfect match for my false indignance.

We make our way straight for the sliding door that leads back into the motel room. It's on a slippery incline that nearly has me on all fours. I fumble with heels caked in mud. Matt slips off his shoes and begins to unfasten his bowtie. I manage to kick the heels off just in time to stop him from getting any further.

"Hang on. Let me."

He gives me a skeptical look. Not reluctant. Just confused.

I feel my smile grow slightly embarrassed. "*What?* I *like* unbuttoning dress shirts. It's hot."

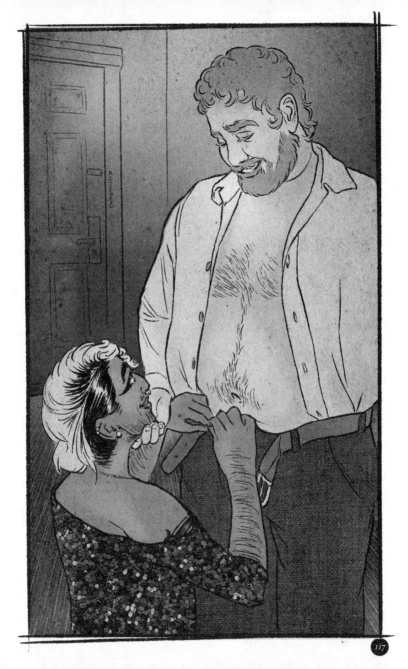

Each button makes a satisfying click coming away from my long nails. The fabric resists me more and more as I make my way down his torso.

I purse my lips. It's the same expression I have when trying to draw a perfectly straight line. And isn't that the natural resting state of my desire? A state of controlled aggravation, deliciously unresolved?

Matt brushes his hand against the stubble on my cheek. I glance up at him. He's chuckling to cover for the inherent vulnerability of being undressed.

It takes similar focus to manipulate his belt prong from the strap. I eventually manage in a single orchestrated gesture.

"Nat twenty," I inform him.

"You had a high dexterity modifier to begin with."

The final button on his pants is pulled almost impossibly taut.

I take this one slowly. My eyes meet his once I think I've got the basic motion in order. Then the rough faux-cotton and button plastic mingle under my fingers, coming reluctantly undone.

I take a deep breath.

He feels his way to the bottom edge of my sequined top. I adjust my position to let him shimmy it up, off my torso, over my head. My arms rise into the air. It feels like a lethargic, deliberate sort of dance. My body weaves—*snakelike*—back into his arms.

"Do you like dancing?"

He winces, as though half-expecting me to pull him into a dance that very minute.

"I'm terrible at it."

"I think you'd be good if you let up your inhibitions. Just be patient with yourself." I grab his dick, and work my hand up the shaft. "You're already so patient with me."

He makes that pleasantly surprised sound. The one that sounds like a laugh and a gasp and a moan all at once.

But to his credit, he can still respond. "Nobody wants to see some fat, nerdy white guy dance. People make cringe compilations about that shit."

"Fuck them. I want to see it."

"Yeah, but you're—*weird*." He says it fondly. I feel his fingers slip under the elastic strap of my briefs. I start to ease out of them.

I'm taking this in stride. *Weird is okay. I like weird.* But—

"I want you to love your body while we're fucking. I want you to love it as much as I do. If you can handle mine—"

"Yeah, but you're *actually hot*. Like heads turn, people-walk-into-street-lamps hot. I'm just some really unremarkable looking dude."

I grin. Naked in the pale, unsympathetic motel lighting, I want him to drink me in with his eyes. I want to feel his thirst. I want him to know that I'm doing the same to him. "You want people to see you and walk into street lamps?"

"I dunno," He really does look uncertain.

"Probably not, but—it would be nice to be noticed *sometimes*. I kind of want to be—*objectified?*"

The word sounds foreign coming from him. Like he's heard it, but seldom used it. "Watching you draw that portrait was awkward. But it was kind of refreshing too."

I reach out to trace the shape of his chest. "Sometimes I wish people noticed me less. That I could just exist in public and be unremarkable as I am."

I trace the rim of his nipples. The shadow where his chest sags. The light trail of hairs leading down his belly.

"But if nobody ever noticed me at all, *I'd hate that*. It's like screaming into a void. Like the feeling of making art no one will see."

I can't live without external validation anymore than he can. Not for all the well-intentioned social media posts about self-love and confidence-building workshops in the world.

"But for what it's worth–" I guide his hand around back. Down past my ass. Between my legs. "I've been a flood plain all night, just watching you move in that suit."

There's a face that people make when they're feeling begrudgingly sexy. The *shame at accepting a compliment that doesn't match my self-concept* face. The *guilt at subjecting people to the sight of me, and actually liking it* face.

He's making it now. "You mean you're not just horny all the time?"

A part of me knows he's joking. But a part of me knows he also kind of *isn't*.

"Hey, *fuck you*." This time, my indignation is real.

"I didn't mean it like that—"

"Yeah I bet." If it takes my temple throbbing to strip him of the delusion that I fuck him because I'm some kind of exotic sex fiend, I *will* flip tables. "I am *not* your reverse trap incubus boyfriend fantasy."

Matt smiles helplessly. "That's a low blow, man."

"Yeah? Well you need to find a way to believe me. Or we're gonna have a problem."

"Alex—" Now he looks frustrated. Rightfully so, I must admit. I may not have acknowledged it yet, but some part of me *knows* I'm having an overreaction.

It's his turn to strip me naked. "Are *you* ever going to believe I like you? *Actually* like you, and not just like to *fuck you?*"

I sit down on the bed. I'm keenly aware my body will leave a stain on the covers, but just now, I couldn't care less.

He sits down next to me. Cautiously, as though he thinks I'm about to push him off. "I offered to drive you here. I wanted to help you with your show. I sent you all those messages about how much I want to be with you. And you still think I don't see you as a real human being?"

I compulsively massage my forehead and breathe in,

       like I'm preparing myself

   to dive off a pier

into murky lake water.

"I'm sorry. I've been letting my fear turn me into an asshole, and I'm sorry."

I turn to him. "What do *you* want to do now?"

Matt is caught midway through preparing to give an apology of his own. I can see it in the conciliatory way he looks at me.

He was hunched over, fiddling with his hands. Now his back straightens. He tilts his head and frowns, as though he's never been asked that question. Maybe it only lives in his own mind. A hoarse, strangled whisper of a question, that breaks through the clamor of his thoughts during long showers and sleepless nights.

"I want *you*, asshole."

I let him take the lead on kissing me.

He wraps an arm around my waist and lowers me down onto the bed. One of those compulsive carrying types, I remind myself. *This box is marked fragile.* **Watch your step.**

Gentle and *fragile* aren't the words I'd use to describe myself, much less what other people do to me.

But I *like* this.

And I have no better words for the way his hands roam across my body. I don't know how else to explain the slow and deliberate way he's kissing me. Or the way his dick is methodically brushing up against my slippery clit.

"He-ey—" I softly lift his face from my neck.

"Yeah?"

"There's this purple dildo in my bag. Could you go find it?"

He raises his eyebrows.

"Don't worry. I'm not replacing you. This is for a good cause."

"A good cause?" He asks, teasingly.

"My personal enjoyment is a *great* cause, I'll have you know."

"Oh, no doubt." It takes him a while. Mine was a rushed packing job. Dress shirts, cheap portfolio binders and mismatched socks explode onto the floor.

He returns with it in hand.

I can see him examining the thing. Purple dildo may have been a misnomer. It's one of those bulbous, fantastical novelties, sculpted as though it might belong in some twisted DM's D&D homebrew where all the monsters roll to fuck.

"You keep a disembodied goblin dick in your suitcase?"

"I thought you might like it."

"Sure." He laughs appreciatively. "So uhh—where do you want it?

"In my front. And I want you in my ass."

"Is that—gonna be okay?" He looks skeptical. Like this is one of those porn things everyday people leave to the paid professionals.

"Trust me, it's gonna be a lot better than okay."

I'm soaked and he's drowning in just how wet I am, so I'm not worried on that account. But I expect Matt to have more questions.

I'm waiting on him to reference the ick factor of anal. Maybe ask me if I'm clean, or insist that I douche first. He *is* looking a little thoughtful.

I begin to get up. "I can—"

"I just don't want to hurt you."

It suddenly occurs to me that I didn't even think to mention a condom. It's as though my mind had already decided I was demanding too much. Pleasure and safety? You can't ask a man to

give you both!

The fact that he was thinking of my comfort first leaves me with a bitter, guilt-ridden taste in my mouth. I can demand more. And I *should*.

"Hey umm, are you tested?" I ask, even as I know how unlikely it is.

This all-too-monogomous guy just out of a three year heterosexual relationship? Why should he bother?

"Actually yeah. Uh—" He looks slightly uncomfortable, "My ex and I both got tested after she had a one night stand with this guy at her graduation party. It turned out later that—"

He sighs, "It wasn't their first time, so she already knew he was good, and we probably didn't have to. But point is, I'm good too."

Oh. "Sorry man."

"It's fine. Really."

I raise my legs up and around his body, coaxing him closer. "But thanks to her being awful, I know we're both good."

"You trust me?"

"Why shouldn't I?" I have a million reasons. Some of them are even quite reasonable reasons, but trust is a choice. I want him to hear me make it.

I reach for his dick and stroke it. "You've been *very* patient with me."

I may not have the hardware to know for sure, but maintaining a semi this long can't be easy. "Why don't you start, and we'll find a good moment for the plus-one somewhere along the way."

I lift my lower back up, pressing my legs into his sides for balance. My hand guides his dick downstream.

I apply a bit of pressure, and he does the rest.

That first moment always feels like a newfound opening. This orifice isn't a constant presence. I feel the head of his cock against it, tenderly insistent.

Then I feel it widen. Making itself known to my body. Reminding me it exists with a sudden, sharp ferocity.

So many men have told me anal hurts. So many women have. And here I am, this strange creature for whom it always just felt more *intense*.

Down there he feels thicker. Harder. Like he's taking up every last bit of space inside me.

In that first instant I'm paralyzed by his entrance.

My lips part voicelessly. I feel an *Ahhgh* building at the base of my throat, but never coming to fruition. When he begins to ride up against me, I feel helplessly overtaken.

Then my breath begins to return. I will myself to push back against him. Timing the motion of my hips with his thrusts.

"Slow. Easy." My vocal chords barely manage that much. They're tied up in moaning my way through several octaves of arousal.

But I've still got room. I just don't feel it yet. It will be several minutes of this tantalizing exercise in self-control before he's local.

Soon enough each thrust will feel intimately familiar. My ass will press up against his balls with the same ease my head reclines against the pillows. His body will be as much a part of me, with every motion of his hips, as I am of him.

"Okay—" I grab his arm. I can't even keep a solid grip before my hand falters, scraping the covers for some relief from this flood of constant, devastating sensation.

He hesitates. But then it's there. Cold. Unyielding, in the way of firm silicone.

It takes something like a *shove.*

I thrust my head back, and cry out.

I'm not in control.

I'm in glorious freefall.

It's sore at first. A raw ache as the hard, unfamiliar texture introduces itself to my insides. Then with one hand, I take the base. And with the other, I squeeze my clit. Flat on my back,

with Matt supporting my legs, I feel *full*. I feel *unbound*.

My nervous system screams.

I'm probably screaming too, but I can't tell.

We're multiple exposures in a single shot. Not truly moving, but somehow caught in a state of every position at once, superimposed on one another in unison.

I'm so aware of how much is inside me. Joy and warmth and nerves like fireworks.

He feels so **big.** And not in the way I can get used to. Every thrust a fresh intrusion. An absolute takeover of my senses. *Every thrust.*

It comes upon me suddenly.

No build-up. Not the usual way. But I can feel the rasping cry in my throat before I even know what made it.

My insides pulse. Bracing contractions. I feel them take shape around him. The dildo slips from my grasp, and forces itself free.

I sprawl. My body feels weak with pleasure.

He's on top of me now.

I barely registered his descent. Snug against my torso. Breathing in time with my wild heartbeat. Somehow, I manage to reach my arms around him. Press him closer. Wrap my legs around his back, even as I'm still quivering from the full-body shock.

His motions feel urgent and impulsive. He's breathing fast. Moaning every time he's at peak depth. Plunging his face into my neck, as though he'll find his solace there.

I've got you. I find my voice again. Breathy and strained, but still very much mine, "Fill me up. You're so close. Go on. Fill me."

My climax is still ravaging my body. I want him to feel it too.

I want to eclipse him in that same bare-knuckled bliss.

He shudders in my arms.

The sound of his orgasm is quiet.

Choking, gasping for air, like he can hardly breathe.

I feel his cock throb. Once. Twice. A third time.

Even as warm as we are, as drenched in fluids as we are, both inside and out—his cum feels bracingly hot. Another advantage, I ponder vaguely, of anal. I can actually feel it. And I don't have to worry about where it goes next.

I break into laughter. I can't help it. My joy needs somewhere to go.

He needs to catch his breath before he joins me.

We lay there laughing. Wheezing. Suffocating in our own sweat.

"Oh god." Matt tries to rise, but his arms betray him. It's those shaky post-sex muscle spasms.

I let him flop back onto me. The rest of his sentence is spoken into my chest. "That might as well be my workout for the week."

"You did good."

"I can tell."

"I mean you have to admit this is more fun than jogging in place at a gym for half an hour. And a lot more cost-effective!"

"Nice." I can feel Matt holding back more laughter. "Thanks for saving me all that money."

"Any time." I pause. My brain is shouting at me. *Get over yourself, Alex.* "Actually—"

"Hm?" He looks up. Something about my tone must have worried him.

"This is gonna sound cheesy, but—that's probably some of the best sex I've ever had."

He smiles. There's a little mischief in that smile, "What, only *some of*?"

"I've had a lot of sex, okay?"

"I'm just saying. I'm not here for the consolation prize."

We could go on like this for days. I'll say something sarcastic. He'll joke about it. I'll throw his joke back at him. And round and round it goes. *Somebody has to take a stand.* "Look I'm trying to say something cute here. Are you gonna let me do that, or what?"

"Okay." His smile wavers a little. "Say something cute. And maybe—*not* about sex this time?"

I'm working up to it Matt. Cut me some slack, alright?

I sigh. Something cute. Yeah. I've got this.

Matt rolls over onto his side and gradually works himself up into a sitting position. With his head cocked to one side, he watches me deliberate. He looks dubious. "Well, don't force yourself."

"I—feel like we could be a thing."

"Yeah?" He answers quickly, without any trace of sarcasm.

"I mean that I want us to be a thing."

"Me too." He's got a shy smirk, as if to add—*in case you didn't know.*

"I know." I've known it for a while.

"So what does that mean to you?"

I sit up, sobered by the maturity of his question. "Uh. Well. Maybe we could make a little more time for each other? I could play D&D with your guys. Maybe stay late to watch some anime. You could come to a party with some of my friends from art college—"

"That sounds alright." He's looking at me with so much fondness it hurts.

Now I'm suddenly all too aware of the bodily fluids congealing between my skin and the covers.

"So you uh—wanna take a shower?"

Matt seems to have simultaneously struck upon the same thought. "Oh yeah."

I shrink from the initial burst of cold water leaving the shower head, much to Matt's good-natured amusement. It's a small bathtub and a narrow stream of water.

And then I find myself shuffling close to him as the water warms us both.

I know the make-up is running down my cheeks.

He reaches for me.

And here we are, pressed against each other between three walls of cold, white tile and a generic floral-patterned curtain.

"This is not how showers work," I whisper.

The proximity of his body feels like a respite from some deep-seated, nameless anxiety. I don't want to let him go.

"I guess it is now." He kisses my forehead. The long, wet hair that's come undone.

"Yeah." I smile, in spite of myself. "I guess."

Epilogue.

A JOURNAL OF MUSINGS AND AFFIRMATIONS

WHAT DO YOU DRAW WHEN **NOTHING** COMES TO YOU?

*T*hese days I often struggle to catch my breath.

It's not that I have nothing to say, or no one to say it to. I'm just stuck. Suspended like a primordial flower in the amber necklaces my mom kept from her life in Soviet Georgia.

"Like they were planted yesterday."

Without my art I feel less real. Preserved, like those Baltic amber beads, in a place beyond time.

A TRIED &
TESTED
SOLUTION:

They drew them on brick walls, street poles and bathroom stalls. Every length, colour and quality of dick. As a kid, they made me giggle, the way you do when you hear a bad word.

Then they made me bitter. I'd check the bathroom mirror, waiting for mine to grow in. Nobody told me that's not how it works.

Now they make me hot, or indifferent. Like any other naked appendage, it's more about the *how.*

SOME DAYS I AM HELD CAPTIVE-

-BY A VAGUE, UNNAMEABLE ANXIETY.

My dad once told me vultures in the Caucasian mountains forage for bones. They'll even eat the marrow.

There are mornings when I feel like a carcass, ready to be stripped clean and devoured.

Everyday tasks hover like vultures, waiting for me to fuck up. Any moment now. Maybe washing the dishes. Or brushing my teeth. I may crawl into bed, but my head won't rest.

I wish they'd hurry up and eat me.

ANXIETY CAN BE MY STRENGTH.

IT KEEPS ME ENGAGED WHEN PROSPECTS SEEM BLEAK.

IT KEEPS ME AWARE WHEN THE TRUTH FEELS TOO HEAVY.

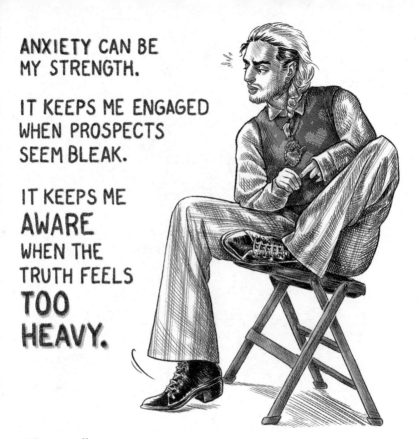

Then it will pass.

The ugly squawking of a thousand worries will dim to background hum.

Like the vibrations of an engine, I'll come alive. Invigorated by the burden of those same anxieties that nearly tore me apart.

Their weight will keep me working. Keep my feet tapping. The music playing. The boiling water in my decanter marinating week old leaves. Every sip of over-steeped tea like a shot of adrenaline straight to the soul.

FEMME IS A PART OF ME.

It used to be hard to dissociate femme from the spectre of the *good hostess* and *future wife*.

Qualities I was praised for while growing up.

They told me my transition would be a waste of a pretty girl. They even wept for my barren womb, as if all that I am would be lost with my capacity for grandchildren.

But I found femme again when I left them behind. I found it at the core of my fledgling masculinity, and nurtured it into a form entirely my own.

Make-up and heels are my armour now.

I feel powerful, standing a few extra inches off the ground with my face painted a sultry mask.

I even feel naked going out without them.

My outfits draw the wrong sort of attention. I know this, and I nearly abandoned them for it. But all the shouted obscenities and gangs of strange men following me down the sidewalk couldn't keep me from myself forever.

IT'S OKAY TO **NOT** BE OKAY

I put on my face on the days I fall apart too.

The foundation will melt and the cheap eyeliner will spill down my cheeks, but I'll feel stronger for trying.

Even if I don't answer a single message, turn down all my social engagements and barely manage to feed myself, let alone get properly dressed, it reminds me that *this too shall pass*.

AND IT'S OKAY TO SOMETIMES DO NOTHING AT ALL.

Work is a coping mechanism to keep me from the worst days.

I find it hard to see my worth without it. My self-respect withers under the influence of those hopelessly long, empty hours.

I've had to learn they aren't all wasted.

I can fill my world with small comforts. These little things that still bring me joy.

I can accomplish nothing, and still be human.

BURNOUT IS NOT FOREVER.

FILL YOUR LIFE, AND THE CREATIVE SPIRIT WILL RETURN.

The longer I work, the more I realize the dreaded *burnout* is an inevitable part of my creative cycle.

Every project is a deep dive. Like any other aquatic mammal, I have to eventually surface for air.

Sometimes the depths are terrifying and the air is sweet.

But I have to seek my nourishment at the bottom of the ocean, alone with my deepest, darkest self.

ALTERNATIVELY... PRACTICE WITCHCRAFT.

So I will always return eventually.

Of course, I *can* get impatient.

The frustration of the empty page and the blank canvas is all too real.

For a truly brutal case of artist's block, I recommend sidewalk chalk, tea candles from the corner store and an isolated parking lot. The translated incantations can be found on early-2000s internet pagan blog collectives.

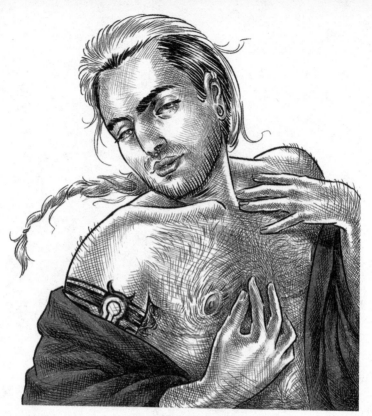

Go wild.

I've heard it described as "mutilation".

Well-meaning cisgender friends have asked me, in hushed tones, whether it was worth it. Strangers have reacted with a mixture of morbid fascination and polite horror.

Everyone wants to hear about the surgery.

They never quite know what to say when I tell them, quite honestly, that it's the best thing I've ever done.

IT'S **YOUR** BODY.

REFUSE THE WEIGHT OF
THEIR PREJUDICE AND FEAR.

YOU ARE ALREADY
CARRYING ENOUGH.

The beauty ideals that haunted my body's first attempt at puberty have grown quieter with every passing year.

I've fallen in love with my thick body hair. My so-called Jewish nose. The traits of a people I hardly know written across my skin for the world to see.

And the traits I've chosen. My flat chest, effeminate voice and rough, permanent stubble. I've come to adore them all in equal measure.

FEW THINGS ARE MORE COMFORTABLE THAN SHARING A BED WHEN IT RAINS.

I've begun to take comfort in the warmth of a familiar body next to mine.

It worries me, but not enough to stop. Instead, I recline in the pillows, silent, letting his proximity deepen, while I try to stifle the fears of how ephemeral it is. Sometimes this even works.

For a moment, I let myself sink into half-formed thoughts of affection.

I let go. I almost feel safe.

"Unnatural", they used to call it.

I never felt myself reflected in the American queers my family feared. They were distantly familiar. Enough to suggest that something inside me was broken.

"A bourgeois disease of Western excess". I was "corrupted".

That never stuck.

Not after I took the first steps to making myself feel whole, and felt, in that moment, more deeply than ever, that I belong to this world too.

I have no love for social media.

The place where myriad faceless strangers thirst after photos of my body. The men behind the avatars, expressing what they'd like to "do to me" under their presumed anonymity.

This virtual flesh market is their playground, but I can tolerate it long enough to profit off their bottomless hunger.

WOULD IT HELP IF I WORE MY CRIPPLING IMPOSTER SYNDROME~

~AS A FASHION STATEMENT? ♥

As long as I maintain separation from my virtual persona—*keeping it real*, but not *too* real—I know I'll make it out alive.

It's more difficult with my art.

The self becomes confused with the piece. Praise and attention confuse my motivations.

I lose time to refreshing pages for likes. Sometimes I forget my reasons without them.

Are artists truth-tellers or clever charlatans?

THERE ARE THINGS I DON'T YET HAVE THE COURAGE TO DRAW.

THEY ARE TOO DARK.

TOO CLOSE.

TOO PERSONAL.

WILL I EVER BE READY?

I think I've become a little of both.

In the end I'm always of two minds.

The one who fears and the one who overcomes. The one who thinks he knows himself, and the one who sheds the past like old skin.

Can I look back at these words without cringing? I don't want to live in the past, but neither can I forget what forged me.

About the Author

Nicholai A. Melamed is a writer and illustrator.

He creates illustrated stories, games, comics and poetry—often dealing with the interwoven topics of mental illness, sex-positive approaches to queer intimacy, and issues of class-based poverty viewed through an intersectional lens.

Many of these projects center trans protagonists on a path of trauma recovery and reconciliation with the spaces they once called home.

His work is an ongoing exploration of resilience at the crossroads of queer, trans identity and ethnoreligious diaspora experience. A place defined by lack of belonging, that nonetheless preserves a gravitation all its own.

Dramatis Personae

About Alex Mazor

Alex is a second-generation Georgian Jew. His parents immigrated from Soviet Georgia to Israel, and later to Southern Ontario, where he was born. He was raised divorced from his cultural heritage while his family struggled to assimilate into a very conservative Canadian Orthodox Jewish community.

Because his family couldn't afford tuition at a Hebrew day school, Alex attended a secular public school instead. There he befriended the local circle of misfits. Fanfiction writers, goth artists and anime otakus, many of whom ultimately came out as queer.

Alex waited on his own coming out until he had engineered an exit strategy. Predictably, it didn't go well. He moved in with his friends, who had just left highschool to attend art college in Toronto. The next few years were a whirlwind of striving for financial independence as a camgirl, figuring out that he was not, in fact, a lesbian, and putting together a portfolio to make it into his program of choice.

Alex began his transition part way through college. It was a long and unstable process, frequently halted by financial need and his family's refusal to give up citizenship paperwork. He was simultaneously developing a small, but committed following as a horror artist. This allowed him to spend less time camming, and more time drawing on camera.

In his third year, Alex was struggling to fit into the social milieu at school, and felt secure enough in the earnings of his online persona to drop out. He said goodbye to his roommates, and moved into a basement apartment on the outskirts of the city. By this point, he hadn't sat down for a conversation with his family in nearly half a decade.

Alex had long avoided developing attachments in his personal life. After one particularly bad relationship with an older patron-turned-partner, he had come to rely on a revolving door of one-night-stands and friends-with-benefits to satisfy the occasional hunger for intimacy. Fiercely obsessed with doing whatever it takes to maintain his independence, he couldn't find it within himself to trust or rely on others easily.

I can only keep going.

Maybe that's the only real choice I've ever had.

It is here that he first encountered Matt.

About Matt Connors

Matt spent his childhood in a small, suburban town north of Toronto. His dad worked as a carpenter, while his mom was a cashier at the local Sobeys. It wasn't a terribly happy marriage, and though he was raised an only child, he was vaguely aware of having half-siblings by another mother.

Matt wasn't a particularly motivated student. He devoted the hours away from school escaping his troubled homelife by playing video games, watching anime, and creating elaborate pen and paper roleplay worlds for his friends. The rest of his time was spent accruing a meagre allowance by working behind the cash register at a local Gamestop.

His ex was a former co-worker who was a year behind him in highschool. Matt stayed in town while she finished her diploma, and his friends dispersed among various city colleges. He ultimately became a full-time store manager.

Matt followed his ex to Toronto as she pursued a degree in the liberal arts. They officially became an item. Her friends became his friends. Their shared one-bedroom apartment in the heart of the city and mutual hobbies were maintained by his steady income.

Several years into her degree, their relationship began to unravel. Where they were once planning their next convention trip or powering their way up an MMO leadership board, Matt now found himself on the wrong end of late night conversations about how his ex needed more freedom to explore and meet other people.

His unconditional support for her ambitions had begun, ironically, to feel stifling. He was safe. A solid foundation from which to pursue her journey of self-exploration while she needed him. But now it was time for her to move on.

Since the dissolution of their relationship, Matt struggled to develop a complete sense of personal identity. Living in his ex-girlfriend's shadow had left him feeling detached from his own needs and desires.

Matt couldn't remember the last time anyone asked him what he wanted in life—least of all himself.

It is here that he first encountered Alex.